Matari

Matari

by Luke Rhinehart

Hart-Davis, MacGibbon London

Granada Publishing Limited
First published in Great Britain 1975 by Hart-Davis, MacGibbon Ltd
Frogmore, St Albans, Hertfordshire, AL2 2NF and
3 Upper James Street, London W1R 4 BP

ISBN 0 246 10811 8

Printed in Great Britain by
Northumberland Press Limited
Gateshead

Every voice is the voice of Buddha
Every face the Buddha face
Every fall of dice the Buddha's way

Oboko

Part One

A beautiful statue
Of the hardest stone
Stands stiffly
In the garden.
Beneath it
A wild flower grows
And dies,
Unseen.

c. 1792, from fragments
attributed to Matari, 1766-96

One

In the mountains above Samika—just to the north of the Kybo pass—lies a small Buddhist temple, abandoned now, as it was then, but used by travellers for shelter from the snows which fell there month after month through the long winter. The poet Oboko had been journeying alone for ten days on his pilgrimage to see his old Master, Eno, in the monastery beyond Samika on Nuni Bay. He was then a young man of twenty-four, of medium height, very wiry and compact. His body had been disciplined to a sharp edge of fitness and strength by many years of physical and spiritual discipline with Master Eno, permitting him to undertake the four hundred miles of his pilgrimage with no more thought of hardship than he might have had during an afternoon walk.

He had watched uneasily the clustering of dark clouds throughout the morning and, at noon, as they released their first tentative flakes, had increased his pace. The winter's accumulation of snow already lay deeply in the low spots and gorges, often obscuring an iced-over mountain stream which skirted the path, a stream whose low murmur of spring could already be heard. By the time he reached the northern point of the pass, at dusk, a blizzard had been raging for four hours and he was exhausted. Squinting painfully through the snow which flung itself across the sky at his back, he followed anxiously the indentation through rocks and pine which he hoped led to the temple and shelter from the storm. Two hours later, when the snow was falling more gently and a half moon occasionally broke through the clouds, he finally saw the dark blur of a building.

He pushed open the ancient wooden door and, after closing it, sniffed for significant odours in the room. As he was noting the faint smell of smoke he saw at the far end of the room a tiny red glow: the remains of a small fire. Swirls of snow were blowing in through unboarded windows along one side of the room and gathering in lovely conical forms along the frozen floor. The only sounds were the creaking of some old rope—possibly attached to an old gong—the occasional ache and slap of a shutter banging in the back of the building, and the noises of the wind hurling itself over, against, and through the old temple.

Oboko moved silently the few feet to the windowless north wall and lowered his bundle of clothing and cooking utensils to the floor. With his right hand he loosened the bindings along the front of his snow-covered cloak and slid his hand in to grasp the hilt of his sword. Without a sound he slowly drew it out from its wooden sheath. When snow melting from his brows and lashes trickled into one eye he had to brush the wetness away. He could see nothing in the room but a fallen beam near his feet and across from him a square of deep blackness which would be the hallway leading to the other rooms. Oboko had stayed in the old temple before on his way to visit Master Eno and knew that most winter travellers preferred to sleep back there in one of the five windowless cubicles.

He crept along the wall to the remains of the fire, near which lay what looked like an empty wine bottle. Squatting, he collected pieces of straw scattered here and there, squeezed them into a long bundle, and held the end of his torch against the bright ashes, blowing twice until the straw fizzled and flamed.

With a suppressed grunt he rose and walked to the edge of the hall, holding the torch in his left hand and his sword in his right. As the flickering light cast quivering shadows on the walls he moved silently to the first room, in which he saw only an old straw mat and some animal droppings.

The second room was also empty, but as he approached the third he heard a noise: a periodic buzzing, like the sound of trapped bees. It was someone snoring.

He glided on to the last cubicle and, his sword in readiness, looked in. As his straw began to burn nearer his hand and to splutter he saw a huge dark bundle lying on the floor. Oboko entered and poked at it gently with the end of his sword. A man began to moan at the touch, a low hoarse 'no, no, no, no'. As his flaming straw burned his fingers, Oboko dropped it to the floor and pressed harder with his sword against the blanket of the dark figure below him. A man abruptly sat up.

'Get away!' the man said loudly, staring wildly at Oboko. 'I'm not ready!'

The face flickering beneath Oboko in the last fitful burning of the straw was terrified.

'Izzi!' Oboko cried, surprised at recognizing the face. 'It is I, Oboko.'

'Get away!' the man said again, pushing himself back against the wall.

'I am Oboko!'

The man stared upwards, his face now barely visible in the dying light.

'Oh, great tongue of Buddha,' he said, 'I thought you were ... With that sword I thought ...' Izzi stumbled awkwardly to his feet and the two men embraced in utter blackness, the larger, rounder Izzi engulfing in a bear hug the slighter body of Oboko, the ice of whose robe cracked and shattered.

'A drink!' said Izzi loudly. 'A drink. Let's go to the fire.'

After Izzi had fumbled in the darkness with his blanket and clothing, the two men strode back up the hall and into the room with the red eye of the fire and the sudden brief sparkling of the drifting snow. Izzi marched over to one corner and returned with some sticks of kindling and some twigs. Soon the fire they sat before was spitting out tongues of flame and providing the first bit of warmth

Oboko had known since the previous night. He removed his brown, snow covered cloak and let it lie close to the fire. At the same time Izzi, sitting cross-legged opposite him, took from inside his own greatcoat a bottle, looked at it with beaming reverence and took a long drink. As he handed it on to Oboko, he licked his lips, smiled, and then spoke.

'I thought you were death himself,' he said. 'But it seems instead you are Oboko.'

'So it seems,' replied Oboko, smiling and beginning to scrape the snow from his pants and boots.

'The gods have brought you to me in the night.'

Oboko smiled. 'A strange and futile thing for the gods to do,' he said.

'Ah, but I am out of food,' said Izzi, 'my horse is rotting somewhere on the plateau, and my faithful servant Raco went away three days ago.'

'But I also have no food.'

A look of fear crossed Izzi's round face, and then he laughed.

'Well, we can quote our poetry to each other as we starve to death. I wrote one of my best poems after a fast of almost five hours.'

He laughed again, folding his hands over his big belly and his eyes twinkling. His thick black hair and beard were tousled, with pieces of straw clinging here and there.

'You look well-fed,' Oboko said, handing back the bottle.

'I just ate the last of my food—a whole rabbit. Never put off to tomorrow what you may eat today.'

'If your servant doesn't return?'

'Then I will become bitter and brood. How bad was the Kybo pass?'

'The wind can still get through.'

'And Samika is impossible until the snow stops. Living Buddha, I think the gods may be serious this time.' They both paused to listen to the sound of the wind hissing and shuddering with little pops at the windows, whining across the roof top and roaring through the frozen pine forest which encircled the temple.

'They can't starve a big man like you,' Oboko said. 'It's the little ones like me they shut up in temples and starve.'

'Ah, 'Boko, you could exist for months on the wind and snow, but I need food, heat, people, the city. I'm going crazy here. I haven't slept in thirty-six hours. My heart beats like a drummer experimenting with new rhythms. It stopped beating completely three hours ago but I hiccoughed and got it going again.'

He laughed. Then turned his face away from the fire and coughed. He was a large man wrapped in an expensive coat, and looked flushed and healthy.

'Izzi, I have known you now for five years and you have been dying steadily and dramatically every hour of that time,' Oboko said, smiling. 'You are also the only man I have known who snores while wide awake. Could you not at least look a little sick?'

'Ah, but I practise snoring only to try to trick myself into falling asleep,' he replied, 'and my appearance is that last flush of vigour that a dying man always manifests just before he expires.'

'A five year flush.'

'I die big.'

They smiled at each other and Izzi absentmindedly took a third gulp from the bottle before handing it back. Oboko fingered it delicately, wiped the opening and took a small amount into his mouth. His features were fine and soft, and his ten day growth of beard looked trim and neat compared to Izzi's great black bush.

'Where are you going?' Izzi asked.

'I ... I'm on a pilgrimage to Samika to see Master Eno.'

'What for?'

Oboko held the half-empty bottle in front of his eyes as if studying it.

'My Lo-Chi died.'

Izzi looked searchingly into his friend's face for a moment.

'Ah, 'Boko,' he said simply.

Oboko paused and began to concentrate on his breath flowing into his belly, into his lungs and ... out of the belly, out of the lungs ... He stared down into the fire. Into the belly ... into the lungs ...

'Fifteen months ago we were riding through the mountains near the River Ossapi,' he said softly. 'She was thrown from her horse. She broke her back.' Snow swirled into Oboko's lap from the cone-shaped mass off to his left; the fire sizzled.

Izzi, now holding the bottle tight against his belly, waited, then asked:

'And were you married?'

Oboko, attending to the rise and fall of his lungs, answered mechanically:

'No,' he said. 'The accident occurred a month before the date.'

Izzi shook his head slowly back and forth.

'I'm surprised,' he said. 'I always thought that you would take the death of anyone, even yourself, with perfect serenity.'

'She didn't die.'

'She didn't die?'

'She ... lived on after the accident for five months. In pain. Unable to move.'

'Lo-Chi ... with a broken back.'

Oboko, staring into the fire and trying to feel the slow rise and fall of each breath, felt again the slash of pain at the image of his betrothed walking through the fields, touching her toes against the surf, smelling a flower, serving him tea: a girl so in love with life that Oboko always wondered that he—hard, monkish Oboko—could possibly share some of her love. And then: Lo-Chi with a broken back, staring at the walls with the blank stare of a wounded, dying doe.

'And then she died,' he said aloud.

'And now you are going to see Eno?' Izzi asked.

'Yes.'

'So he can explain to you death?' Izzi asked and an almost contemptuous expression passed over his face.

'So ... I ...' Oboko looked up at Izzi. 'At first when she lay helpless in bed I controlled my breathing, my feeling. I visited her, but I didn't feel or show my grief or my bitterness. Lo-Chi did. She raged against the fall, cursed the Gods, wept each evening like a child. Not I. I didn't share her rage or her tears, but stayed steady as a stone. Until she ceased raging, ceased weeping.' Oboko paused, his eyes moving sharply away from Izzi's to stare off at the darkness. 'The last two months she simply stared at the wall.'

Izzi held his bottle respectfully against his belly without drinking while Oboko spoke.

'And then she died,' he said again.

'Yes,' said Oboko.

Izzi frowned into the fire and took a long, loud drink from the bottle.

'Well,' he said. 'I told you so. Never invest yourself or your heart in anything outside yourself. Keep them invested in something safe, sure, like poetry, or death. Me, my motto is, "Never give to any woman any more than six inches." He laughed. 'In exceptional cases, when I'm spiritually inspired, six and a half.'

Oboko was staring into the fire without an expression, counting his breaths.

'Ah God, 'Boko, what a time I've just had in Mamisha. They published my series of poems on the seasons and I was the toast of the court for a week. Had women dangling from my armpits. And food! Great Buddha's balls, I ate so much venison one night I had to sleep alone. No woman could get past my belly to my crotch to do anything.'

He laughed once and then turned his face away from the fire, coughed and pulled his greatcoat tighter against him.

'I almost died. I really did. The doctors tried to pretend it was indigestion but I know. I know. The heart. My heart almost beat out its last little ditty that time.'

They both sat up a little straighter when a shutter which had been banging once regularly every six or seven seconds briefly banged three times, almost like a knock. Then the noises which were their silence resumed.

'What had brought you to Mamisha?' Oboko asked.

'Ah, I was paid a year's wages for writing a series of poems celebrating the beauty and grandeur of the great family of Muffli. Ever heard of the great family of Muffli?'

'No.'

'Neither had I. But they must be great since they could afford to pay me a year's wages. And they chose *me* to celebrate their grandeur. Wealth *and* taste.'

Izzi was drinking steadily now, his face flushed, his hands shaking slightly, his smile vaguer and less intense than earlier.

'But now, now, 'Boko, now I'm on my way to Samika to write for the Lord Arishi.'

'Ahhh,' said Oboko.

'"Ahhh" is right,' said Izzi. 'Arishi has promised me three times what Muffli paid. Everything I write there will be shown at the emperor's court. And the Lady Arishi is supposed to be the most beautiful woman since Mara the temptress.'

'You have arrived,' said Oboko.

Izzi snorted out a laugh.

'Not quite. I'm stuck in an abandoned temple in a spring blizzard without food and almost without booze.'

'It is the calm before the storm of your triumph.'

They listened together for a moment to the wind howling outside in the trees.

'If this is the calm,' Izzi said with a look of fear on his face, 'Buddha protect me from the storm.' He heaved a deep sigh and stared into the fire, his back sliding down a few inches against the wall.

'And you, 'Boko, what have you been doing?'

'I write my little poems.'

'And . . . ?'

'I read my little poems.'

'And . . . ?'

'And you and my friends read my little poems.'

Izzi snorted again.

'Smart man, 'Boko. They can't cut off your income.' He laughed crookedly, at whom Oboko could not tell.

Soon Izzi dozed off, his body slumped awkwardly against the wall. Oboko rose and went off to get Izzi's mat, finding another in the last cubicle for himself. He settled Izzi flat beside the remains of their fire, the empty bottle held against the side of his chest. He fixed his own straw mat against the north wall and then, as he did each night before retiring, no matter how exhausted, assumed the lotus posture to meditate.

For a long time—he always assumed it was exactly fifteen minutes—he sat erect breathing regularly, keeping himself awake, thinking nothing, hearing the wind, sensing the snow still steadily dancing through the windows in front of him, hearing the rhythmic buzz of Izzi's snoring, the occasional predictable clatter of the loose board or shutter somewhere in the back of the building, noticing the sporadic clean, clear blocks of moonlight on the frozen floor, and feeling, always feeling the smooth, sensuous rise and fall of his flat stomach and chest as he breathed. Abruptly, when his body assumed that the quarter of an hour had passed, Oboko rose and walked to the corner of the room near the door to take from his bundle there a small piece of paper, ink, and a pen.

He prepared to write a poem. Every evening now for almost four years he had written a poem before sleeping. Some of them were very bad, especially in the last fifteen months; some were good. He never knew what he was going to write about until it was written. Usually he wrote *haiku* or *tanka*, but sometimes, even though beginning when exhausted, he had written for over an hour a poem of many lines. At other times he had taken over two hours to write a *haiku*. But always, always, he wrote a poem before retiring.

In the darkness Oboko's pen etched out in his neat, tiny handwriting the words he could not even see:

> The wind and the moonlight and snow
> Even the snores seem frozen.
> Fireflies dart in the darkness,
> And die with nowhere to go.

He looked at the words, frowned at the self-pity submerged in the last line, sighed, wanted to write the poem a second time, but decided he was too tired. He placed the pen, ink and paper back in his bundle, rolled over on to his mat, and drew the single blanket up to his neck. He felt the rush of sleep falling upon him like a black sword when he heard a noise. He heard a horse whinny.

The back of his head jerked four inches up off the mat. Through the noises of the wind against the temple and through the unboarded windows, he heard again the neigh—it was a shriek—of a horse.

He threw back his blanket and went to the door. His exhausted body resisted the simple effort of opening it to the storm outside. He stood there listening. Only the wind. He pulled open the door and gasped as the cold air slashed across his face and pushed his body backward. Then he thrust himself forward and staggered out into the night.

'Hai!' he shouted.

Only the wind answered back, with its own long-drawn 'aaiiiii i ii'. No one could possibly be coming up from Samika against this storm; it must be someone coming through the pass. His body ached with the tension of having to move out into the cold and wind, but he moved, lifting one heavy foot after another through the two feet of snow towards the bend in the trail leading up to the pass.

'Hai!' he yelled again.

This time, from behind him it seemed, he thought he

heard an answer, a sound. Turning around and going now with the wind, he forced his legs into an awkward trot, stopping after twenty paces to shout, and then plodding further forward.

He stumbled and fell. Rising, it was the horse he saw first, a mound of darkness in the snow. Then the smaller blur of darkness beside it. He fell on his knees beside the horse and reached for the human figure which lay sprawled beside and partially beneath it: a woman, eyes closed, face only a blur. One foot lay under the horse, whose breath came in rapid labouring gasps. Oboko dug with his fingers into the snow around the woman's legs, deeper and deeper, until at last able to free the pinned foot. Hands stinging, eyes blinded by a few whiplash flakes, he lifted her into his arms and stumbled back towards the temple. For a moment, when he had gone many paces without reaching the building, he thought he was lost, but pushing forward the dull grey mass emerged and he entered.

His arms were trembling as he lowered her beside the red remains of the fire. He reached inside each of her riding boots to see if moisture had entered, and when he felt the icy dampness he snarled, his teeth chattering. He removed her boots, rubbed her tiny feet with his hand and wrapped them in his blanket, Izzi snored.

He gathered what twigs and straw he could, and the last of Izzi's kindling they had been saving for the morning, and built up the fire. With his fingertips he gently brushed the snow away from her face and hair. Her face, he saw now in the flickering light of the fire, was strangely peaceful, rather pretty, her breathing regular. As he prodded with his finger at the last of the snow on her neck he was startled to notice a necklace and, looking now beneath the masses of black hair, earrings too. The silk of the garment about her neck was expensive. He reached a hand tentatively inside her clothing around the shoulders and upper chest, again to check for moisture, but here the flesh was dry and warm. When he sought in his mind for another blanket for her, he remembered that the horse outside had two large travelling bags attached to the saddle. After standing magnetized to the bit of earth where he stood, he finally, feeling like a helpless flake of snow being blown about by the wind, went out again into the storm.

The horse when he found it this time lay still; its breathing had stopped. When he dragged to the temple the two bags he found them almost useless: inside were two other silk gowns, a cotton robe, undergarments, some perfumes, a bag of jewellery, a wallet with hundreds of bills, a large hand mirror and a notebook. There was one small woollen over-garment and this Oboko spread across her, with the dresses piled neatly on each side. She opened her eyes.

Oboko stared. So alive and beautiful was the face created by the revelation of her opened eyes that he was stunned. The human thing that had been only a wearisome task he'd had to deal with was miraculously transformed in that moment to a woman, so abruptly beautiful that Oboko realized he'd experienced the transformation like a slap across the face, a slap which had awakened him from—or was it into?—a dream. He became aware after several moments that her large soft eyes were searching his gravely as if examining him for signs of illness. There was no trace of pain and bewilderment in her stare; only intense, alive interest.

Oboko could not speak; in his mind no thoughts flowed. He stared.

Her eyes glazed then for a moment and a slight frown appeared on her brow. Her lips trembled as if trying to form words. As Oboko watched, her eyes exploded once again into that acute vital attention, and she spoke softly and in awe:

'I didn't die,' she said.

Their eyes explored each other's as if creatures from different universes were meeting for the first moment. Finally, the woman's lips and face were transformed by the slightest and most ambiguous smile—at being alive? At Oboko?—and her eyes, as suddenly as they had opened, closed.

The moon, after flooding the room with its miraculous light, was buried again behind the clouds; Oboko was now staring at a barely visible human bundle. He adjusted the clothing around her once more and, as he worked to protect her neck from the cold, felt a slight shock when he first touched the masses of hair that lay there. The long silken strands seemed to sweep endlessly around her head and shoulders and arms and Oboko became strangely uneasy, as if the hair were alive. He pushed a cloth scarf next to her neck and stood up.

Enough. Yes, enough. She was apparently uninjured; the fire and his blanket would warm her; she should be left to sleep. He hurried away to his mat against the north wall and curled himself tightly inside his cloak. Enough. Had he forgotten anything? As he lay there in the cold, shivering, he had the feeling that something was yet undone. After lying awake for two minutes without thought entering his mind, he uncurled, went to his bag, pulled out ink, pen and a fresh piece of paper and wrote:

> The head and body dying,
> All falling snow.
> The opened eyes:
> Alive.

Whose head? Whose body? But in a few minutes he was asleep.

Two

Lo-Chi was falling down the side of the mountain and Oboko with long leaps and slides was trying to overtake and save her, but her body tumbled and twisted and fell and he could not reach her, his own body slipping from control and banging against the rocks, banging again Lo-Chi falling, Oboko grasping, his shoulder being thumped from rock to rock falling falling his shoulder ...

''Boko, 'Boko!'

Izzi's excited face leaped before him; Izzi's hand was shaking his shoulder.

''Boko, a miracle has occurred, or am I still drunk, I don't know which. Come quickly.'

Oboko sat up drowsily, Izzi pulling at his arm to move him towards the fire.

'A woman, a beautiful princess, beside the fire. Look.'

Oboko, rubbing his eyes, staggered up beside Izzi and off towards the sleeping woman.

'I see nothing,' Oboko said sleepily.

'Look! Look! There, a woman!' Izzi whispered hoarsely. 'Look at that hair, that face!'

Oboko looked at Izzi with a bewildered expression, then directly down at the sleeping woman. He was glad her eyes were closed. He wondered why he felt like playing this strange game.

'Izzi, my friend, there is only a fire and some rags.'

Izzi was bewildered.

'Only ... only a fire ...'

He looked incredulously at the beautiful sleeping woman, then dropped to his knees beside her.

'Oh,' he said, 'Oh, 'Boko ...' His pudgy hands reached out and caressed the air around the sides of her face. 'I thought I had died in the night and when I awoke, my heart not beating, and saw ... I thought ... was sure ... one of those Christian angels ... a lovely, lovely ...'

'Stop playing with your hands Izzi,' Oboko said sharply. 'We need more wood for the fire.'

Izzi turned to stare up at Oboko, his eyes narrowing as if in cunning. Standing, he looked for a sign of playfulness on Oboko's serene, cold face, but there was none. Oboko beckoned Izzi to follow, watched him glance sadly back over his shoulder as at some scenic view that would soon be lost forever from sight, and then they proceeded towards the outer rooms in search of wood. They had just entered the hallway when from behind them in the main room they heard a gasp. Turning round, Oboko hurried back beside the gaping Izzi: standing next to the fire with Oboko's blanket held in front of her was the woman, her eyes open, alive.

'Ah, 'Boko, you liar,' said Izzi, striding forward happily. 'Welcome to reality, lovely lady. I am Izzi, the poet-laureate of Mamisha, and this is Oboko, the poet of the wind.'

She stood slender and still, her face cold. Her silence and stillness made Izzi stop abruptly halfway to her.

'I ... am ... Matari ... Matari Tariku, of Samika,' she said hesitantly.

'And what brings you to our religious retreat in the mountains?' Izzi asked.

'I ...' she looked now for the first time that morning at Oboko; as during the night before, her eyes searched his intently. 'I am on my way to vacation in the south,' she said. 'My retainers lost me in the blizzard. I thank you for saving me.'

'Oh, we didn't save you,' Izzi said. 'Buddha took care of that. What can we do for you?'

'Nothing at all, I am fine.' She pulled Oboko's blanket closer to her. 'But ... but ...'

'But you'd like to dress yourself for the day,' said Izzi. 'Oboko, let's go and chop down a forest for the lady's fire.'

A second time they walked out into the hall and this time went down it to look for fuel for the fire. The old temple, abandoned for over forty years, was built mostly of wood, so travellers down through the decades had taken to collecting their firewood from the partitions, frames and beams. Whatever past beauty the temple may have possessed had been eaten away by the human insects, who arrived, bit out of the building enough for warmth, and passed on, leaving interior walls like skeletons and unboarded windows like mouths open to suck in the wind. Although the main meditation room had also been ravaged in this way, Oboko chose to take wood only from the back rooms.

'I'm glad she turned out not to be a dream,' Izzi said, as they began choosing partitions from which to tear loose boards.

'Realities are more trouble than dreams,' Oboko replied frowning.

'Who cares,' said Izzi, smiling.

Ten minutes later when they returned to the meditation room, each with an armload of short split boards, the woman stood quietly with her back to them looking out of a window. The snow could be seen still falling softly outside and occasionally flowing lazily in past her face. Some flakes were planted like little ephemeral jewels in her black hair, which fell in thick waves down her back to her waist. The woman was now wearing her boots and a blue cotton dress which flowed almost to her ankles. She was shivering.

When Izzi let his load of wood crash to the stone floor she turned to them, seeming relaxed and unafraid. When her eyes turned towards him Oboko looked away, taking his armload of kindling up to the ashes to prepare to build a fire. While he began raising his sword and slamming it down on to the ends of wide boards to create narrow splinters, Izzi was busy wrapping Oboko's blanket around Matari's shoulders and spreading Oboko's cloak for her to sit on. When she was seated he began taking the kindling and building a fire. Through all his attentions Matari remained silent except for the simplest of replies to his courtly questions. After twenty minutes, Oboko had prepared all the wood and gathered snow from the mounds beneath the windows to put in his small earthen pot. Izzi's blazing fire was soon boiling the melted snow in preparation for their making use of some of Oboko's tea leaves.

Oboko, however, found himself bothered by the heat of the fire. The room seemed strangely crowded, stuffy. He wasn't thirsty.

'I must collect some additional wood,' he said, standing up.

Izzi and Matari both looked up at him, Izzi beaming, Matari attentive, neutral. Oboko turned and went out again into the cold hallway.

*

When he returned twenty minutes later dragging two five foot sections of a fallen oak beam, Izzi and Matari were still seated by the fire but now chatting gaily, eyes bright, with Izzi's big black cape now draped over her slender shoulders, and Oboko's blanket now around Izzi.

'Where have you been, leper?' Izzi shouted, 'while I have been tending this magnificent fire.'

'And I have prepared a breakfast,' said Matari.

Oboko placed his two logs against the wall and joined them for a breakfast of biscuits, sweets and tea, all except the tea provided by one of Matari's unnoticed bags. She and Izzi were already drinking, and Matari now poured tea into a copper cup and handed it to Oboko. Their eyes met and she smiled that same ambiguous smile of the night before. Oboko frowned, thanked her and sipped at the hot liquid.

'Madame Tariku is a member of the great and glorious Arishi clan,' said Izzi. 'She married one of the cousins.'

'In a spring blizzard all families are the same,' said Oboko, and flushed at his rudeness. 'I'm sorry,' he added immediately. 'I don't know the city of Samika.'

Matari looked at him alertly for a moment, and then away.

'The family of Arishi is rotten with the disease of honour,' she said.

There was a silence.

'But you told me—I've heard they're the wealthiest and oldest and most noble family in Samika,' said Izzi.

'They are,' said Matari. 'They have a rich, old, and noble rottenness, which in the name of honour corrupts all.'

No one spoke: Oboko sipping at his tea; Izzi poking at the coals; the woman staring coldly past the fire at the wall.

'What do you mean?' Oboko finally asked softly.

'I do not wish to speak of it,' Matari replied.

'But still ...' Izzi mumbled almost to himself, 'but still ...' and then loudly, 'they show very good taste in picking women for their wives.'

Matari smiled politely.

'Do you think,' said Izzi, 'that Lord Arishi will let me compose poems celebrating the greatness and antiquity of his family's rot?'

Matari did not smile. Oboko sipped at his tea. Looking into the fire he abruptly asked her:

'What happened?'

Matari did not answer.

'She was on her way to Lissa,' Izzi said, 'for the spring flower festival. When the blizzard struck she was separated from her retainers.'

'Was your husband with you?' Oboko asked her. She

was still staring coldly at the wall between the two men. She again didn't answer.

'Her husband is going to join her later. He—'

'What happened?' Oboko asked quietly, his eyes on the fire, his heart beating rapidly.

'What do you mean, "What happened?"?' Izzi said irritably. 'I just told you.'

Oboko looked up at Izzi, who glared at him fiercely, and then over to Matari. He was trying to control his breathing.

'A lady travelling with retainers doesn't carry her own clothes and money.'

Izzi looked quickly at Matari but she didn't move or speak.

'What do you mean ...?' he asked.

'A lady travelling with retainers doesn't get separated from them no matter how bad the blizzard.'

Now no one spoke. Without wind, the trees and shutters and ropes were silent. Only the fire made its accustomed music.

'I only ask to help you,' Oboko said.

Matari turned to him and her eyes were attentive but cold.

'I need no help,' she said.

'She doesn't need help,' Izzi said aggressively.

Oboko met her gaze for a moment and then looked away.

'We all need help,' Oboko said.

'You wish to help me?' Matari asked.

'Yes.'

'Find me a room where I can be alone.'

Oboko searched her eyes for some other message but received none.

'Yes,' he said, and rose and left.

*

At the far end of the hallway was the entrance to the Master's room. Invisible in the darkness of the night, it was hidden by wooden debris and a massive stone slab once part of an old oven. Oboko knew the room had been closed up because of some superstition regarding the last Master's manner of dying in it. He pushed away a few boards and ducked under the stone slab. Inside he began brusquely trying to clear the chimney and to cover over the broken panes of the two windows. He found he was irritable. He wished the snow would stop so he could get on to Samika and the monastery and Master Eno. When he returned briefly after an hour's work to get a knife from his bundle he saw Matari and Izzi still seated by the fire looking very solemn. Although Matari raised her eyes and looked at him gravely, Izzi poked at the fire.

Later still, when he went to have an afternoon meal, Matari was alone in the main room. He stopped noiselessly to watch the light from the fire dancing softly on her pale skin as she stared at the flakes of snow drifting lazily in the window. With Izzi's heavy black cape over her shoulders the soft material of her gown seemed even more feminine and delicate. When he moved into the room she started, looked at him for a moment with fright, and then smiled politely.

'Where's the great poet Izzi?' Oboko asked.

'He has gone to bury my horse,' she said, her smile disappearing.

'Ahhh. Yes. But that's very difficult in this weather.'

'He was my personal horse and he saved my life.'

'Ah. Yes.'

When Izzi returned the three of them had a second meal together, Izzi and Matari doing most of the talking —primarily about the brilliance of the people who lived in Samika and some famous poet whose work Oboko had always particularly disliked. There was no talk of Arishi rottenness or of Matari's husband.

In the late afternoon Oboko started a fire in the Master's room and Izzi and Matari transferred themselves there where their talk, perhaps heated by the warmth of the room, became more lively. Matari's brown eyes flashed with merriment and she often matched Izzi's wit and poetry line for line.

After the sun had set Oboko returned from checking the weather to hear Matari singing. Her voice as he approached the room seemed to him to have a somewhat artificial quality to it that he didn't like. He stopped in the doorway and watched her as she completed her song: kneeling erect, her hands folded in front of her, her chin raised, she was singing to the wall above Izzi's head. Izzi was sprawled in front of the fireplace. When she'd finished, he applauded loudly, his eyes blazing as if he were drunk.

'Great Buddha's bliss, but you can sing,' he exclaimed. 'Incredible! Angels would be shamed into silence.'

Oboko's eyes met the glittering black eyes of Izzi for a moment—was Izzi laughing behind those eyes, at Oboko? at Matari?—and then Oboko decided to boil some snow in the main meditation room and, alone, have a cup of tea.

Three

'That woman is trouble,' Izzi whispered gloomily. Matari had been left to fall asleep on a mat beside the remains of a large fire in the Master's fireplace; Izzi and Oboko had retired to the main room. It had been warmer in the afternoon, almost near the melting point, but the snow, like some permanent, unending flow of nature, still fell. It blew in little clouds through the windows, as if white curtains were being billowed occasionally by the wind. Oboko was sewing a tear in one of his two cotton shirts. Izzi was licking longingly at the mouth of a now empty bottle.

'Trouble. I know the type.' He glanced at Oboko and played with the neck of the bottle in his beard. 'She'd be trouble if she weren't an Arishi and, with that thrown in, she's double trouble.' He sighed. 'I can't afford to play games with the wife of Lord Arishi's cousin: not at six thousand yen a year.'

Oboko poked the needle into his shirt, drew it through and poked again.

'As a mistress she'd be all tears and trouble,' Izzi went on. 'I bet I'd have to hear about every bit of her husband's family's rot since Buddha, in between each lay.' He rubbed his behind back and forth across the floor twice and spit into the fire. 'You know ... I didn't tell you this, but ... she told me this afternoon that ... she's run away from her husband.'

'Obviously,' said Oboko.

'Why obviously?'

'Ladies don't carry small fortunes. At least not with their husband's permission.'

'She's got a *lot* of money?'

'Yes.'

'Ah, Buddha, triple trouble. She not only gets caught tummy to tummy with some nobleman, but runs off with a fortune.' He groaned and looked up at Oboko frightened. 'Great hump of hell they must have sent an army after her!'

'Is that how she put it, "tummy to tummy"?'

'Oh, no. She said and I quote: "A nobleman was very kind to me, and my husband became violently jealous."'

'And you read that as "tummy to tummy"?'

'Naturally.'

'Well, it's all right. An army will kill us quickly.'

Izzi groaned again.

'They may come here tonight,' he said. 'I may be holding the last bottle of my life this very second. And it's empty!'

'As long as the blizzard continues, no one is going to leave Samika to try to come here.'

'And when it stops snowing?'

'When it stops snowing, we will bid the lovely Matari farewell and descend to the city.'

The two men looked at each other.

Izzi sighed.

'And so pretty. Such lovely teeth! Such eyes!' He smiled at Oboko. 'Come, 'Boko, you're no prude. Let's both seduce her. We'll do it in rhymed couplets.'

Oboko looked back at Izzi without expression.

'Who shall write the first line?' he asked.

Izzi laughed.

'Let chance drop her where it will,' he said. Oboko didn't smile, but turned back to the fire.

'But she's flat-chested,' Izzi went on, becoming gloomy again. 'I'm sure she must be flat-chested.' He rolled the bottle wearily along the floor away from him. 'Flat-chested and trouble and coming at a cost of six thousand yen. There's always that to keep me chaste.' He hauled himself to his feet, grunting. 'I'm going to go to sleep again in my back cubicle. How about you?'

'I'll stay here again. I like to hear the wind and watch the snow.'

'Well . . .' Izzi looked sombrely at Oboko for a moment and then flashed his devil's smile. 'May the warmth of spring visit your dreams!' he said.

Oboko smiled back.

'And the sweat of summer yours,' he replied.

'Not likely,' said Izzi.

After Izzi had left, Oboko set about washing their dishes in melted snow and placing them near the fire to dry. He took off the shirt he'd been wearing and used it as a rag to wash. His chest, arms and abdomen showed not an ounce of extra flesh; when he paused once to stare into the fire, his body's hardness flickered in the firelight as if he were an oiled bronze statue. Then he put on the cotton shirt he had repaired, his brown cloak, and the tiny beaded necklace with the small carved wooden Buddha which he always wore against his chest. He pulled his legs into the full lotus posture and sat for fifteen minutes silently trying to close his mind to the flow of the universe. He was totally centred on the fire, flying through space on the red carpet of coals his eyes were fixed on, when the fire suddenly disappeared and he imaged Izzi and Matari lying side by side laughing. He grunted and yanked his mind back to the fire, but it wouldn't stay.

Unable to meditate, he arose and prepared for sleep. He adjusted his bundles and placed his wet shirt nearer the remains of the fire and rested on an elbow with pen and paper. His poem came quickly and he wrote it without thinking and without an afterthought.

> Twig after twig feeds the fire.
> All the coldness of my room
> Cannot resist.

Before he had settled his blanket around his neck he was asleep.

Four

He was awakened in the morning by some noise, he didn't know what, and lifted his head to see Izzi's broad back blocking out the light from the near window. The fire was out. It was very cold and fear reverberated briefly through Oboko like a roll of thunder: why, he didn't know.

'It looks like it may clear,' Izzi said from the window.

Oboko rose, rubbing his hands together under his cloak, and moved to beside Izzi and looked out. Although flakes of snow still fell lightly, the sky was brighter than it had been in days. Sunlight could be seen spilling down on to the trees on a ridge off in the distance. The previously fallen snow lay on the ground, the outbuildings and the serene green of the fir trees like tranquil crystal armies at rest after a long march. Although it seemed to be colder, there was no wind, and the sun occasionally slid through the clouds above to send lightning dancing from the fields of white.

'Now we can leave,' said Oboko.

'No, we can't,' said Izzi.

'It looks like it will stop soon and remain clear long enough for us to make Samika,' Oboko went on mechanically. 'It's only eight or ten hours away going down, even without horses.'

'It's a two day walk up through the pass to the next shelter.'

'Who's going through the pass?'

'We are.'

'We've just come through the pass.'

'We wish to revisit its beauty.'

The two men stood side by side staring out at the snow, their breaths puffing out by turns in front of them with rhythmic regularity. Neither looked at the other.

'Matari is being chased,' Izzi said gruffly. 'Her pursuers come from Samika. It is our duty to save her.'

'It is?' Oboko asked with an intentional child's innocence in his voice. He realized he both loved and hated Izzi for wanting to help Matari.

'Some would consider it our duty to turn her over to her husband,' Izzi said, 'but we are poets.'

'You are a poet about to give up a year's riches and honours from the famous Arishi family.'

'Riches and honours are nothing to the beauty of her eyes,' replied Izzi gravely.

'Still, she is flat-chested,' said Oboko with great solemnity. But as his words struck the cold air, he wished he hadn't spoken them.

Izzi was silent for a while and then turned away to walk towards the fire.

'We must eat well,' he said. 'We must prepare enough food for the journey in case the weather clears and we dare try to make it up the pass.'

'Is Matari awake?' Oboko asked softly from the window.

From behind him he heard Izzi fussing with one of the bundles.

'She's awake. I told her we'd have breakfast ready in thirty minutes.'

'Biscuits and tea?'

'I'm going out now to chop up that damn horse. I need meat.'

'But I thought Matari asked you to bury her horse.'

The two men turned simultaneously and looked at each other for the first time that morning.

'If I'd buried the horse,' said Izzi, his black eyes expressionless in his bearded face, 'I might as well have buried all of us with it. Where's the axe?'

Oboko got Izzi the axe and, after Izzi had left to chop up some breakfast, collected some kindling and one good-sized log and built a fire. He was on his knees manoeuvring a few sticks into the flames beneath the main log when Matari entered the room.

She was dressed, remarkably, not in the heavy blanket-capes reasonable in such cold, but in yet another lovely silken gown, white again, as if about to appear at a formal dinner preliminary to a ball.

'Good morning, Oboko,' she said, smiling.

'Good morning,' he said. 'Aren't you cold?'

'Yes, I am. I came to be near the flames.'

Oboko spread one of his blankets on the floor near it. As Matari knelt down gracefully beside him, she turned her eyes with their serene attentiveness towards him, smiled again her ambiguous smile, and in a seemingly unbroken motion lowered her dark lashes and swung her face to accept the heat of the flames from the burning wood. Trembling, Oboko received her glance again like an awakening slap and pretended to be engrossed in feeding sticks in under the log, but finally said:

'Izzi says that someone is pursuing you from Samika.' He hesitated uncertainly and then shot out the next word, as if to get rid of it: 'Why?' His body tense, he dimly realized he ought to be practising his breath control.

'My husband, Lord Tariku, feels it is his duty to kill me.'

It took Oboko a few seconds to say the word again but finally it passed his lips cautiously, as if trying hard to avoid stirring up trouble.

'Why?' he asked.

'A gentleman of the court was kind to me,' she answered quietly, 'and my husband has become violently jealous.'

The words echoed in Oboko's mind and he found himself having to suppress a pained smile. His attention still focussed gravely on the fire, he went on.

'Was there no one in the court to defend you?'

Matari's voice became even softer with each reply.

'There were many to defend me.'

'And they couldn't sway your husband?'

'My husband is a mountain. Mountains do not sway.'

'He's going to kill you?'

'Yes. I was warned by a courtier. I escaped with two faithful servants, but ...'

The fire hissed as some snow, melting from the top of the log, began dripping into it.

'We became separated in the blizzard, and I ... I was lost ...' her voice trailed off, then finished with soft distinctiveness: 'Until you saved me.'

Oboko, his hands now idle in front of him, watched the fire. He didn't dare turn his head to look at her.

'Were there no gentlemen to help you escape?' Oboko sensed the woman stiffen beside him.

'There were many,' she answered with an edge of coldness in her voice for the first time. 'But I would not dishonour my husband by fleeing with the aid of another gentleman.'

So unexpected was this reply that Oboko turned to look at her and met her eyes looking at him with a serene dignity that was close to disdain.

'And was a gentleman kind to you last night?' Oboko found himself saying.

Matari's face retained its coldness for a moment and then surprisingly softened.

'You are a fool,' she said. She continued to look into his eyes, as if searching for the sources of his folly, and then she flushed with anger.

'You are a *rude* man,' she said and, lips trembling, averted her face and turned herself away from him.

'I come with our salvation!' announced Izzi loudly as he exploded open the door and came stomping across the floor carrying against his chest a burden that could only be a huge chunk of Matari's frozen horse.

Oboko watched as Izzi approached the fire and saw

Matari, whose head was lowered and turned away from him, slowly straighten and look at Izzi and his burden.

'What ... what is that you have?' she asked.

Izzi stopped a few feet away and looked gravely down at her.

'Madame,' he said huskily. 'We must soon make a very long and dangerous journey to the south through the Kybo pass. It is essential that each of us have strength so that we may ...'

'Aaahhgggggghhhhh!!!'

Matari's scream was remarkably harsh and unfeminine and she bounded up, struck Izzi an incredible blow across the face, and ran head down with little short steps from the room. In tears.

Izzi, still looking extremely grave, let his eyes meet those of Oboko. The side of his cheek where he'd been struck was red, even into his thick black beard.

'Trouble,' he said, and he plopped the frozen meat down near Oboko and the fire. 'Knew it from the moment I saw her first open her eyes.' He drew his sword, raised it up high and plunged it down into the meat. 'And not a drop of saki to dull the pain.' With the sword end buried almost a foot into the meat—it was a thigh as far as Oboko could tell—Izzi raised up the sword and meat and held them over the fire. 'But I'm damned if I'm going to break my Buddha balls to save a lady in distress unless I have meat.'

Oboko began laughing then, slowly at first, the humour bubbling down deep in his tummy and flowing upwards, shaking his lean hard body and bringing tears to his eyes.

'She won't come with us anyway,' Oboko said after awhile, having to suppress his laughter.

'Why not?' asked Izzi, his eyes already brightening as the meat sizzled and popped and the blood, melting, began to drip into the fire.

'She told me she wouldn't dishonour her husband by permitting a gentleman to help her escape.'

'Oh don't worry about that,' Izzi said, not bothering

to turn to Oboko. 'We're not gentlemen. We're poets.'

'So?' said Oboko.

'It's an old and rich tradition among the governing classes: poets, like other servants, don't count.'

Five

'What will you do if my husband's men come to kill me?' Matari asked Oboko after they had been sitting alone and silent before the fireplace for almost half an hour. All day the snow had been teasing them. It had fallen lightly, then ceased. As they began their final preparations for beginning the journey southwards through the pass, it began falling again. Later it diminished to light whimsical flakes aimlessly fluttering earthward, but again, as they discussed leaving, it began to fall faster. Because of the partial clearing and because it was only a day's ride up the mountain from Samika, Oboko and Izzi had agreed to keep watch alternately a hundred yards below the temple, at the high point which overlooked the path up from Samika. Beginning at noon, each had left the temple for two hours to sit in the cold wind and gusts of snow to stare down the mountain at the winding indentation of bare, windswept rock which marked the trail up.

'I don't know,' Oboko answered after a long pause. 'I don't know clearly why your husband feels justified in killing you.'

Matari brushed her hair away from her eyes. She was looking at him sternly.

'You know nothing, but you disapprove of me.'

'Not knowing, I cannot judge.'

'I shall tell you,' she said. She had been sitting erect, but now she leaned back against the wall. She sighed.

'I shall tell you,' she repeated. She again brushed hair away from her face and, head back, eyes directed off at the old beams of the ceiling at the opposite side of the room, she went on:

'The court of Arishi, to which my husband belongs, is the oldest and wealthiest of Samika and of the southern kingdom. Consequently, it is, for a woman, a bejewelled prison.'

Matari paused, but Oboko, watching her, did not comment.

'The wife of an Arishi lord, even a second cousin, lives only to exalt her husband. This is of course true in all places, but in the lesser courts, where standards have crumbled, there is more freedom. A woman of the court of Ikkosammi in Nugisuko, for example, being unimportant, can, paradoxically, do things which a lady of the court of Arishi ... cannot.'

Oboko saw no expression on her face other than that of an instructor of history giving a lesson. He noticed that this afternoon she was no longer wearing either earrings or a necklace, and she occasionally pulled her red cape about her as if she were cold.

'I was born of the Iridu family and educated to dance, to write, to sing, to dress, to ride, to do things that only the most talented women can do. And then when I married ... it was expected that I cease to dance, to write, to sing and to ride—except for my husband. Except for my lord.'

She paused. When she went on she had sat forward again and looked directly at Oboko, her eyes filled with anger.

'You don't know prison. You don't know what it means to spend your time with brainless children—other women—when once or twice a week, at some court ceremony or performance, you meet men with minds, talents, wit, poetry ... And I could meet those minds, match the talent and wit, value the poetry, but then the excitement and challenge is immediately removed with the public event which occasions it. And even there my ... forwardness was often resented. By tradition, the wife of an

Arishi is expected to excel in only two things: beauty and silence. If you have poetry or song or wit or skill, you may express them to your husband—when you are alone. When he's lecturing you on his latest military triumph.'

When she said nothing for several seconds, Oboko said:

'You speak of the way the world is.'

She glanced at him and sneered.

'Yes. I speak of the way the world is. It educates me to a dozen arts to win the favour of a man and, having won him, it tells me to decorate myself outwardly and enclose my other arts forever in silence.'

'It is the way of the world,' Oboko said again.

Matari's head rested against the wall and she was looking away across the room with eyes that seemed to be glistening with tears.

'Had I been content to bathe myself in trinkets for a lifetime, I would live,' she said softly. 'But I sang to another lord; for that I die.'

Oboko hesitated, but then said:

'Singing is a form of courtship.'

'I will not be silent,' she replied in her subdued voice.

When a gust of wind thrust against the door they turned to see if Izzi was returning. After a moment Oboko asked:

'Could not your husband understand?'

Matari was playing gently with strands of her hair which fell to her waist in front of her.

'Do you know of the Lord Arishi?' she asked.

'No. But why do you ask of him?'

'The Lord Arishi is a proud man. He believes he has the most splendid court in the kingdom. He himself excels in all things: the horse, the bow, the sword ... Against the Nanniwasis in the last war he alone killed ... he killed many men. He believes he has the most beautiful and best wife. You ... you have not heard of her?' Oboko shook his head; Matari went on: 'His court must be the best. The wives of his relatives must be the best. A falling off of one of his family or their wives is a personal insult.'

'His anger, rather than that of your husband, pursues you?'

'They are the same. All the Arishi are the same. My husband is a pygmy compared to Lord Arishi and when the lord frowns my husband kills.'

'For singing ...' Oboko said softly.

'Oboko,' Matari said with sudden feeling. 'I only want to live.'

'Yes,' said Oboko neutrally. She wanted freedom, a freedom absolutely forbidden by tradition, but he did not feel he could judge. They sat together listening to the wind wail around the walls of the temple and watched snow explode briefly through a crack in one of the windows Oboko had boarded over, and settle to the floor.

'And for that he is coming, he is coming, even now he is coming,' Matari said softly. Watching her, Oboko saw for the first time that afternoon that beneath all her defiance she was frightened. The hands that played with the strands of hair in her lap were kneading it tensely.

'How do they know you came this way?' he asked gently.

'I left with two of my female servants,' she said slowly, not looking at him. 'When the blizzard began we were only a third of the way up the mountain. I knew if we continued we would all be lost in the snowstorm. I ordered the two women to return to Samika.'

'Ahhh,' said Oboko. He searched her face for pride, but saw only a hint of a smile, as if the memory were amusing. 'And you went on alone?'

'I can ride; they were ... women.'

'I see.'

'I knew this temple, I knew I and my horse could find it,' she said, the defiance momentarily returning. Then it disappeared and she added softly: 'And if I didn't, I could give myself to the snow.'

'And your women will tell your husband where you went?'

'It doesn't matter. As they return they will have left in the fresh snow enough of a trail to point the way.'

'And thus we will soon have visitors.'

Matari turned slowly to look at him.

'And you, Oboko?' she said. 'From what do you flee?'

He flushed.

'From nothing,' he said. 'I go on a pilgrimage to see Master Eno.'

'Master Eno? You're a disciple?' She turned and drew her legs up beneath her long dress to sit cross-legged facing him.

'Yes.'

'He is a very wise and witty man,' Matari said. She leaned forward and held her hands near the fire. 'But his disciples seem stuffy.'

'He isn't training people to be court clowns,' he replied.

'No,' she said, looking up at him, silent and serious. 'And you, Oboko, are you a great poet like Izzi?'

'No,' he said. 'Certainly not a great poet like Izzi.'

'But though I had not heard your name, he says you are.'

'Izzi plants poems in books, on letters to great lords. I plant poems on the wind.'

'If you are a poet, you should try to find and hold an audience.'

'No,' said Oboko. 'I plant, but where my seeds are carried by the wind I do not care to notice.'

'Oh you don't!' said Matari, tossing her head back and smiling mischievously. 'What a romantic child you are!'

'Thank you,' said Oboko, flushing again.

'I suppose your indifference to success is a sign of your detachment?'

Oboko, feeling ill at ease, as if any answer would be wrong, replied:

'Yes, it is.'

'And do you feel you must come to control all your feelings?' she asked, smiling again her ambiguous smile.

Oboko hesitated a long time, brooding over the image of himself sitting serene and cold at the bedside of his dying, raging Lo-Chi, her anger and grief and frustration swirling around his immobile, formal self. He remembered her stonelike the last month before her death. He remembered parables from the *sutras;* he knew stonelikeness was not proper detachment; he remembered breath control; he tried to remember nothing.

'No,' he finally replied. 'It's rather a case of having no "self" left to have control or have feelings.'

'Oh, you serious Buddhists!' Matari exclaimed, still smiling. 'Eternally freeing yourselves from "self"; everlastingly seeking detachment and control.'

'Well?' said Oboko.

'Corpses are superbly detached, quite completely controlled. I sense little "self" in a corpse.'

'That is not the same.'

'With some of Eno's monks I find it hard to tell the difference,' laughed Matari.

Oboko too smiled, although a part of him knew that it was at him that some of the laughter was directed. When he saw the corpse in himself he felt a great sadness. He knew there was more detachment in the bright play of Matari's eyes than there was in his rigidly controlled breathing.

'It is strange,' he said. 'In our society women are forced to be more controlled than men, except, of course, monks.'

'Yes,' said Matari, seriously. 'Perhaps that is why I have so little enthusiasm for your "control".'

'It's not control,' he replied, smiling at her, 'I know that. We ... I am trying to realize the complete unity of everything, the insignificance of any *one* thing, and thus the end of any need for control.'

'Matari will always be Matari; Oboko, Oboko.'

'We are one,' replied Oboko.

'Are we?' said Matari, her eyes laughing into his so that he flushed and looked away.

'Philosophically speaking,' he said.

'Which is perhaps why I find philosophy often irrelevant,' said Matari, 'although your Master Eno is much freer from it than his monks.'

'He is freer from everything,' commented Oboko.

'He, unlike his disciples,' she went on, her eyes seeming bright with joy or mischief, 'seems to know that purifying the mind and becoming detached has nothing to do with will-power or control or the insignificance of any one thing.'

'I'm not sure,' said Oboko, frowning.

'The story is told,' went on Matari, 'that one day a serious and dedicated monk went to Master Eno and said: "Master, I have an unconquerable problem: I am continually being distracted from my meditations by my desire to make love to almost every woman I meet."' She paused to smile at Oboko, then went on:

'"That is a very serious problem indeed," Master Eno is said to have replied. "And there is only one solution."

'"What is it?" asked the monk.

'"You must make love to almost every woman you see," the Master replied.

'"But Master ..." the monk began to protest, but Master Eno interrupted him.

'"But be very certain," he concluded, "that you are not distracted by your desire to be meditating."'

Matari smiled at Oboko at the conclusion of her little parable. Oboko laughed.

'Yes, that is very good,' he said. 'And you are right: the wise man is unaffected by the storm not because he stands rigid as a rock, but because he rides the wind.'

Matari, still smiling, slowly shook her head, her large eyes watching him intently.

'Ah, but Oboko,' she said, 'the parable was not about storms but about thoughts of women.'

'Same thing,' said Oboko.

And now she laughed in appreciation.

'You are the poet of the wind,' she said to him, 'and I haven't yet heard a poem. I hope you're not becalmed.'

Oboko looked back at her and saw that her face had returned to its expression of quiet attentiveness.

'No,' he said.

'Please recite me a poem.'

A tiny gust of wind puffed a cloudy swirl of smoke back into the room into their faces and for a moment both had to turn away, Matari coughing. Oboko realized that he was pleased with the thought of her wanting to hear a poem but a little fearful that it would all turn out 'monkish'.

'About what?' he asked.

'Well ... I don't know. Let the wind blow where it will.'

Oboko stared into the fire and then recited the poem that for some reason leaped to his mind:

> A leaf, thick-veined, brittle, dry,
> Weakened by the chill of winter's breath,
> Loses its grip on the trembling limb
> And falls to the frozen earth, and death.
> I step on it.
> Do you hear a cry?

When he had finished reciting he looked over at her and she met his serious glance for several long moments.

'Yes,' she replied softly. 'Yes, I do.'

'But why should it cry?' asked Oboko. 'The budding, the blooming and the winter's death are all part of the same flow.'

'Still,' said Matari, and now she was pensive, 'flow or no flow, when we die, we scream or we cry.'

Oboko was silent.

'That was lovely, Oboko,' Matari went on, looking up at him. 'Please let me hear another.'

He smiled.

'Every now and then,' he said, 'I achieve total and

complete enlightenment.' He laughed. 'And then, somehow, in a day or a week, I lose it. During my periods of ... enlightenment, I ... the "I" disappears and ... well, I once wrote a poem.' He gazed into the fire and then recited:

> The moon's the same old moon,
> The flowers exactly as they were,
> My mind still goes on my mind,
> Yet see me glimmer on the pond
> And waver, yellow, in the wind.

When he had finished he could sense Matari watching him, but could feel no hint of whether she liked or disliked the poem. Then he remembered he wasn't supposed to care.

'You are ...' she began softly, '... the poem was ... is ... is beautiful.'

Bright with pleasure, Oboko sat erect, staring with fierce dignity into the fire.

'Why, Oboko,' Matari went on softly and hesitantly, 'have you so ... avoided me since you ... saved me?'

Oboko, surprised by the question, wasn't able to look at her. He arose from his seated posture, his knees stiff and painful still from his long journey, and walked over to the boarded-over window. Looking through one of its many cracks he saw that only small isolated flakes of snow were falling.

'I've avoided you,' Oboko found himself replying in a low voice without turning, 'because a part of me is ... afraid of you.' He slowly moved to face her.

Her eyes met his warmly for a moment and then she frowned and turned away.

'It was a silly question,' she said. 'Please forgive me.'

'Part of me ...'

'Please,' she interrupted. 'Let's speak of something else. Of my singing.'

He could see that for some reason she was dragging

the conversation back to the impersonal and knew that he was relieved.

'I've heard very little of your singing,' Oboko answered. Matari had leaned forward and was poking a stick at the fire.

'It is hard to make you Buddhist poets like the traditional songs of our island,' she said in a low voice. 'We are romantic, where you are hard. We are vague, where you insist on the concrete. You feel we are missing reality, and I feel,' and here she glanced up at him with a soft smile, 'that you are missing life.'

'Where is there not life?' asked Oboko simply.

'Where there is stone, where there is rigid control, where there is no heart.'

'All is life.'

'So your mind tells you,' she said, looking up at him intently, 'but your heart, your feelings, your passion: they are still blind.'

'I don't want to know anything about passion and confusion and torment,' he said, standing rigidly before her. 'If I did I wouldn't be Oboko.'

'Would the universe crumble?'

He suddenly laughed and shook his head at his own coldness.

'No,' he said, smiling. 'But Oboko might. Oboko flows with the wind, and strong winds are hard to ride.'

Matari smiled back at him and replied in a low voice.

'You'd be blown over by a puff.'

'I could ride a hurricane and not muss my hair,' Oboko said, half in self-mockery.

'We shall see,' said Matari.

'We shall?' asked Oboko, beginning to pace back and forth across the small room.

'What the future brings, the wise man does not pretend to know,' she said. 'But stop pacing and sit down. I would like to sing.'

Oboko stopped. They looked at each other, Matari now serene and unsmiling.

'I would like to sing you a *magari,*' she went on as he seated himself opposite her in front of the fireplace. 'Would you like to hear it?'

'I'd be very pleased and honoured.'

'I respect your opinion. I know I don't sing well, but I think this *magari,* which I composed myself, has a certain ... charm.'

She adjusted herself on her knees on the mat in front of the fire and pulled a bit of her dress closer about her neck. Her face became more serious. She clasped her hands in front of her and then took them apart to place them palms up on her knees. She began singing.

Oboko was startled. Her voice seemed to have an immediate power and complexity which in the short song he'd heard her singing to Izzi it had lacked. Her voice flowed effortlessly through a strong masculine opening to a kind of love duet, and as it passed to the feminine altered its quality smoothly. It was beautiful. As the song continued the words and characters took on a depth solely from her voice. Oboko became absorbed.

He remembered little of the actual story—the usual something about a princess doomed by a jealous lover—but the melody and words of one lyric near the end of the *magari* seemed to flow into the room with a magical power: 'Our lives are entwined ... like the veins of one body ... pouring into one another ... mingling like grape vines ... heavy with growing fruit ... laden with a wine ... not kegged anywhere ... Hurry! Hurry! Even now the dark connoisseur ... enters the hall ... to taste us.'

She was looking at him, her eyes bright, her face glowing. Oboko suddenly realized that the song series had ended several seconds before. He felt his mouth must be hanging open, or that he was smiling stupidly. Finally, he said:

'That was beautiful.' He stared at her. 'I am a poet without words ... before the beauty of your song and of your singing.'

She searched his face for a long moment and then instead of smiling, turned away.

'Thank you. Oh, thank you. I'm glad you liked it.'

'It ... it ...'

'I think one or two parts are good, but I know my voice is not strong enough for the masculine mimes.'

'You handle it all as if ... as if you knew every moment what was needed and why. You really have an extraordinary talent.'

'Now you are being a flatterer,' she said and at last she sparkled with joy.

'Being wordless, I jabber on.' He could not tell whether she had felt how moved he was or simply accepted his compliments as she had the hundreds of others she must have received.

'No, you never jabber. You always speak what is in your heart.'

'I lie like everyone.'

'Thank you ! ! !' she said and bounced up with a mock-insulted expression.

'But not about your singing,' Oboko said hurriedly.

'You little boy,' she said, smiling down at him from a few feet away. 'The only one you ever lie to is yourself.'

'Thank *you*.'

'And I imagine you're not even very good at that.'

'Matari ...' Oboko said in a low voice. She stared at him, and for several moments they looked at each other intently, their faces controlled, ambiguous. 'Your name: I felt like speaking it,' he said.

'You say it nicely,' she replied softly.

'Yes, doesn't he?' came Izzi's loud voice from the doorway.

Oboko's hand leaped to his sword and Matari jumped back a step.

'Peace, peace,' said Izzi, brushing some snow off his greatcoat. 'I am not the avenging husband.'

Oboko stood up.

'What ... what do you have to report?' he asked.

'Oh so much have I seen!' sighed Izzi as he clomped into the room, stamping snow off his boots and still brushing it from his coat. 'But on the trail from Samika ... nothing.'

'Good,' said Oboko.

'I don't know,' said Izzi, coming up now beside the other two. 'I fear I may begin to get lonely here. I may actually welcome fresh companionship.'

'You will have it soon enough,' said Matari. She was looking at him coldly.

'Most likely. I'm afraid I must report that during my whole watch it seemed to be clear over Samika, even as it snowed up here.'

'They are coming,' Matari said.

They all stood awkwardly looking down at the fire.

'Yes,' Izzi finally said. And he beamed his teeth-glittering smile, and added:

'How interesting it all is!'

Six

Although Oboko was officially standing his watch, and his eyes were focussed on the trail winding up the mountain from Samika, it is possible he would not have noticed an advancing army. His mind was ricocheting randomly: from the joy of remembering how pleased Matari seemed with that last poem to the torment of worrying about where Izzi had slept last night and what he was doing now back within the temple, and from there to the confusion of trying to feel that he didn't care. He was agitated, anxious, ecstatic, tormented, confused, and, above all, alive.

Even as his heart silently chanted 'Matari' the way it had once been trained to chant *namu amida bussu*—the name of Buddha—he realized what madness it was even to think about her. She was being chased by men intent on either killing her or carrying her back to her husband. Were his feelings primarily of lust, life would be simple; God had created relatively simple means to satisfy lust. But Oboko's feelings didn't know what they wanted. He felt invaded by some foreign substance so powerful that a hundred minutes of breath-counting—actually he'd had to start more than seven times before reaching a count of ten—didn't seem to have the slightest effect. He groaned aloud and, startled by his groan, at last laughed at himself.

'A geisha from Samika,' he said aloud out into the air of the twilight, 'and I am acting like a boy.' As a method of forgetting all about her, he attempted to imagine Izzi at this very moment making love to her, but the effort filled him with such absurd rage at Izzi that he had to stop.

He managed to control himself sufficiently to look once more downwards at the trail winding up from Samika but it seemed to be empty. No snow was falling and the late afternoon sun gave him a good view; the upper half of the path, at least, was empty. But still, sooner or later, the future came. And what then? But Oboko, sitting so erect and stern and immobile on the ridge overlooking Samika, was lost, drowned, unthinking in the infinite unfathomability of Matari's eyes.

*

Much later that evening when Izzi returned from his watch on the ridge and lowered himself opposite Oboko in the main room, his scabbard and sword struck awkwardly against the stone floor. Izzi muttered something, adjusted the scabbard into his lap and looked over at Oboko.

'Matari?' he asked.

'She is sleeping in the Master's room,' Oboko replied.

'Ahhh.' Izzi's expression was carefully blank, but then his wide mouth spread into a grin and his eyes, bloodshot, gleamed at Oboko.

'The wind has shifted,' he said.

'Is it still snowing?' Oboko asked.

'The snow will always fall,' Izzi said. He frowned and pushed the scabbard off his lap into a position alongside his leg. 'And the wind will shift again.'

'Your watch passed quickly,' Oboko said, aware that Izzi had returned at least an hour earlier than their agreement called for.

'In this darkness now I couldn't see anyone coming from Samika until his horse was pissing on me.' Izzi looked angrily at Oboko. 'We're doomed. If they come and find Matari, we're all doomed.'

'It will save us having to climb back through the pass.'

'Easy for you to say. But what have I got to die for? I'm a great and famous poet, and to die now, at the very height of my irrelevancy ...' He grinned and gleamed. 'Ah, 'Boko, that it should come to this: waiting to die for a flat-chested whore.'

Oboko smiled softly. How happily absurd indeed it all seemed.

'You do not have to die for this lady,' he said to Izzi.

'Nor do you.'

'I don't plan to,' Oboko replied quietly.

Izzi wasn't smiling; his eyes watched Oboko's carefully.

'She has lovely brown eyes, hasn't she?' he said.

'Like pools aswim with brown moons,' said Oboko neutrally.

'Or a swamp aswim with dung.'

Both sitting erect, the two men watched each other, their faces stonily impassive.

'Yes,' Oboko said, smiling again. 'That too.'

'Ah, 'Boko, I love Matari and would that you love her too.'

'Oboko does not love,' he said, frowning.

'Cruel 'Boko. How cold is your heart. While the rest of you melts all over the floor.' Izzi smiled. 'Ah, 'Boko, I love Matari and feel I may have to play the vengeful husband and kill you.'

They were both absolutely still. Oboko was listening to a shutter banging.

'Not until tomorrow,' Oboko said. 'I must write my evening poem first.'

'Of course.'

Izzi broke their conversation by turning towards the fire and grimacing in pain. He coughed twice.

'Ah, 'Boko, we're fools, we're fools. Tomorrow we must go down to Samika and give up our folly.'

Oboko didn't answer. He watched as Izzi grimaced

again and put a hand to his side as if in pain.

'I'm dying ... that damn horsemeat ...' Izzi muttered. 'You and Matari starving to death ... I'm dying ... and we all sit on a mountain waiting for that damned dwarf death to lean forward and touch us into "zzzt".' He coughed twice and spat fully and accurately into the fire. Oboko remained impassive. 'We're fools, 'Boko,' Izzi said again, looking up.

'We do what we must do,' Oboko said.

Izzi sighed, and replied:

'Day by day we do our very best and, consequently, make a total mess of things.' Izzi stirred, grasped the middle of his scabbard, and arose to his feet with a grunt.

'I'm going to bed, old friend,' he went on. 'Can I count on you to remain here for the night?'

Oboko watched him without expression.

'I shall remain here for the night,' he said.

'How nice!' Izzi exclaimed with exaggeration. 'And I will be engaged in serious work, so please don't disturb me.' He paused. 'Until I'm about to die.'

'Where shall I find you?' Oboko asked.

The two men stared evenly at each other.

'I think I shall try the Master's room tonight,' he said. He glittered out his smile. 'It's *my* turn again.'

After a silence Oboko said:

'And if someone comes ...?'

'Oh yes. It is a dangerous night,' he said, still grinning. 'I shall have to unsheathe my sword.'

'Don't lose it.'

'Where I'm putting it, it won't get lost.'

Izzi beamed; he wheeled and disappeared down the hallway.

Alone, Oboko began counting his breaths. He had failed six consecutive times to reach ten without his mind wandering when he became aware that the fire was dying. Outside it seemed to be clearing again, for moonlight flooded in through the unboarded windows and the wind blew only air. It was time for a poem. He took out his paper and pen and ink and placed them in front of him. He looked for a moment into the red coals of the fire. He moved his pen to the paper. But nothing came. A shutter banged in the distance. No words of poetry came. He groaned aloud. Still, he must put down something, even if it were nonsense. Slowly he let his pen scrawl out words.

The sky over the city is clear.
The moon shines a path to her door.

He stared blankly at what he'd written. Sighed. He scratched out the words, scratched until not a single letter was visible. He tried again.

A flake of snow
Blown by wind
Into the fire
Falls. Ssst.

When he turned his head at the rush of wind, the three men were already standing inside the huge door, barely visible in the almost darkened room, but unmistakably there, unmistakably there. Oboko, unmoving, kept his eyes, adjusting to the blackness outside the ring of his fire, upon the invaders.

'Welcome,' he said in a quiet voice. Were there signs of Matari's presence here in the room? He sensed none.

'Are you alone?' asked the tallest of the three blurred figures at the end of the room. Oboko felt his body become a degree more rigid.

'I am the poet Oboko on my way to Samika with the poet Izzi. And you?'

The tallest of the three, a large man, moved towards the fire, a long sword on his hip, a shorter one at his belt, a bow over his back. The two men who moved behind him on either side were armed the same, but without bows.

'We are samurai in the court of Arishi,' the tall one

said, and stopped ten feet from the coals of the fire. The other two stopped behind him at either side. One was as young as Oboko; the other old, his wizened face etched with furrows like a walnut.

'Welcome,' Oboko said. 'It's a bad night for travelling.'

'Is there a place for horses?' the tall one said. His face could be dimly seen now, fine-featured with dark eyes. There was still snow unmelted in his hair and beard.

'No,' Oboko answered. 'You'll have to bring them in here.'

The leader made a gesture and the old samurai left to go outside.

'Where is the other?' the tall one said.

'Sleeping. He's drunk.'

'How long have you been here?'

'Two days.'

The tall man turned when the door was opened again, and he waited wordlessly as the samurai brought in three horses, stamping and shuddering to remove the snow, and tethered them to the broken beam near the door. The leader then moved, powerful but graceful, to the fire, and dropped down to sit on his heels and stare across the coals at Oboko. His dark face and eyes searched Oboko's neutrally as he brushed, lightly with one finger, the snow from his slightly greying beard.

'Why didn't you go down to Samika today?' he asked.

Oboko smiled.

'My friend Izzi believes he is dying. He refused to leave this morning.'

'You said he was drunk.'

'He wants to die happy.'

The old samurai who had taken care of the horses joined them and deposited kindling on to the coals of Oboko's fire.

'We are looking for a woman,' the tall one went on. 'A lady. She was lost in the blizzard.'

'Lost in this storm?' Oboko asked. He shrugged his shoulders as if the question were ridiculous.

'She was last seen heading up here, towards the Kybo pass,' added the smaller man, who stayed always just to the right and behind the big one. He was young, younger than Oboko, and his eyes moved constantly over Oboko's clothes as if searching for something.

Oboko poked at the fire.

'Two nights ago a horse came riderless to the temple. We heard its cry, but since its leg was badly injured we killed it.' Oboko looked up at the tall, straight-featured man opposite him, whose dark eyes met his with cold attention. 'There was no sign of any rider.'

The tall samurai now seated himself lotus fashion across the fire from Oboko, adjusting soundlessly his two swords to lie one stretching behind him and the other on his lap. As they adjusted the long sword's lacquered wooden sheath, the man's hands seemed immense. The sword itself was unusually long, over four feet it seemed, and its hilt sparkled in the firelight with some kind of stone or jewels embedded there.

'Yes, you killed him,' the man said.

'Yes.'

'It was the great horse Konlo. We saw his remains outside.'

Oboko blinked once.

'Ah yes. My friend Izzi has a large appetite.'

'If Konlo had been separated from his rider he would have returned towards Samika.'

Oboko tried to look back evenly. He was aware of the clank of a sword as the old man, who had been moving silently about the room, apparently hit something behind Oboko. The sweet odour of horse dung arose from the end of the room where the three horses, still restless, stood. Oboko was vaguely aware that they were now feeding on something.

'Perhaps the lady passed here northward and lost the horse somewhere in the Kybo pass?' Oboko suggested.

'The horse has fallen facing up the mountain.'

'That was careless of him,' Oboko found himself saying, as he concentrated hard on matching the tall samurai's relentless gaze.

'There was no trace of any of the lady's possessions,' the leader went on. 'Had she fallen from the horse, the bags would still be attached to the saddle.'

'She must not have fallen.'

'True.' The eyes of the tall samurai pinned Oboko to his place. 'She probably decided it would be easier to carry her own luggage and walk.'

'I know nothing about it,' Oboko said.

For a full minute the two men simply stared at each other. Finally, although Oboko was aware of no signal, the young samurai, who had been squatting beside his leader, silently gathered up five or six pieces of straw at his feet and thrust the ends into the fire. After the straw was lit he held the torch for two seconds towards Oboko's face, then finally arose and moved off towards the hallway behind the older samurai.

'I ...' began Oboko, but could think of nothing to say. They would either find the obscure Master's room behind the stone slab, and in it Izzi and Matari, or find no one and wonder what had happened to Oboko's drunken friend. As a liar Oboko was proving a failure.

When the two figures had disappeared into the hallway, the young one with the torch, and both carrying their long swords in their hands, Oboko returned his eyes to the leader, who, motionless, relaxed, gazed without expression across at Oboko.

'Why do you seek this lady?' Oboko asked.

'She is lost; she must be found.'

'She didn't go off riding *alone*?'

'She did.'

'No servants?'

'No servants.'

'A courageous lady.'

'That is one of her attributes.'

'And what are her others?'

The samurai leader, the melting snow now flowing

down from his hair across his face like sweat, did not answer. Oboko sensed that he was listening for sounds from the hall. As Oboko too now focussed his attention in that direction he heard muffled shouts being exchanged. Neither Oboko nor the samurai moved, but Oboko became aware that at some time his antagonist had eased his legs out of the lotus so that he was ready to move. Oboko's face was covered with real sweat. The indistinct shouts had ceased, and now they heard the sounds of footsteps coming up the hallway towards them. Oboko's legs wanted to spring to action but he kept them still. His eyes wanted to turn towards the hallway, but he kept them looking neutrally at the man across from him, who also, seemingly serene and uninterested, looked back at Oboko. Torchlight could be seen out of the corner of his eyes flickering from the hallway. The noises indicated that the footsteps were now actually within the room.

'Is it time for morning meditation already?' came Izzi's loud, disgruntled voice.

Both Oboko and the leader turned to see Izzi standing between the two samurai, looking sleepy-eyed and dishevelled.

'Where is the lady?' the leader asked sharply.

Izzi blinked open-mouthed at the leader and at Oboko.

'What lady?' he finally asked and began rubbing the back of his head and yawning.

'The lady who came with the horse.'

Izzi stumbled over a blanket and, as he righted himself, glanced again at Oboko, who, expressionless, turned his head sharply to the left to look at the horses standing in a cluster near the door. The movement was as close to shaking his head 'no' as he dared.

'The only thing that came with that horse was a load of biscuits,' Izzi answered. 'Stale biscuits.'

The leader turned his head sharply to the young man, who had again dropped down to a position just behind and beside him.

'Did you look in all the rooms?' he asked.

'This man was in the last cubicle. There is no sign of anyone else in the temple.'

'Lady Arishi is not here,' added the old man.

'Lady *Arishi*!' Izzi blurted out.

The three samurai all looked at him.

'Why does the name surprise you?' asked the leader.

'I ... I ...' Izzi, standing slump-shouldered a few feet from Oboko, shook his head as if to clear it. 'I am the great poet Izzi and have been called to serve the Lord Arishi at his court. Is it *his* wife who has fled?'

For a few seconds no one spoke.

'Fled?' the tall samurai asked slowly.

Izzi stared back at him and let his mouth hang open stupidly.

'"Fled,"' he said. 'Samurai don't go searching for solitary women unless the woman is running away.'

The leader scrutinized Izzi.

'For a drunken, dying man awakened from sleep, your mind works rather well.'

'I may be dying,' Izzi replied and straightened himself. 'But I'm not drunk. I'm the great poet Izzi.' He seemed to be puffing out his chest.

'Yes,' said the leader. With another tiny gesture—this time Oboko was able to notice it—the old man, short, thickset, moved off through the blocks of moonlight to the horses and began digging into the travelling bag for something. In a few seconds he returned with rice cakes, fruit, dried fish, and two wine-skins. He went back a second time and returned with earthenware cups. He squatted again beside his leader near the fire and opened the first wine-skin.

'So you are the great poet Izzi,' said the tall man, and for the first time he smiled at Izzi, who had flopped down between him and Oboko.

'You have heard of me?' asked Izzi, beaming.

'The Lord Arishi has ordered you to his court. You must be great.'

'Exactly!' said Izzi, and he accepted with a larger smile the cup of saki offered him by the old man.

'You must be great, or come cheap,' went on the leader. 'The Lord Arishi doesn't like to pay too much for court poets, fools and other hangers-on.'

Izzi frowned into his cup.

'Izzi is not a fool or a hanger-on,' he said.

'We are all fools, and if you are being paid to hang around the court you are a hanger-on.'

'Then you too are a hanger-on,' Izzi said, looking up aggressively.

The three samurai all laughed.

'Oh yes,' the leader said, drinking deeply of the saki. 'But a captain of samurai is paid ten times what is paid the poet.'

'Killing is always more profitable than creating.'

'Probably because it is more interesting, more human.'

'Probably,' said Izzi, pouring himself some more.

'Let me hear one of your great poems.'

'I only recite for noblemen.'

'Do you?' said the leader, smiling and reaching his cup to the old man at his left for a refill. 'Then how honoured I am that you will recite for me.' Still smiling, he took out his short sword and, with a casual, unexpected swish, chopped off a half-inch of leather from the toe of Izzi's left boot.

No one else moved.

'Feeling that I am short enough already,' Izzi said softly, looking at his boot, 'I would like to recite a poem.'

'How nice,' said the leader.

'It is about samurai.'

'A worthy subject.'

'Samurai and death.'

A brief silence.

'A natural combination,' said the leader.

Izzi straightened up and drew his feet back under him.

'It is rather long, but brilliant,' he said.

'From the great poet Izzi one can expect no less.'

'"Death and the Samurai,"' Izzi announced. He cleared his throat again and began, his voice soft, firm and dramatic:

> We see him swallow ants in the morning fire,
> Crush crickets with an indifferent foot,
> Wither weeds with the noonday sun,
> Impale a hare upon an arrow's shaft,
> And yet, as we stalk our enemy
> Through the evening's fading light,
> Hushed for the sound of a leaf's crack
> Or sleeve's light touching of a bush,
> We do not see him as he squats,
> Hungry and set, upon our back,
> Waiting to eat again.

The fire crackled softly in front of them, its light flickering over the faces of the five. The leader, his face now gloomy, looked into the flames.

'You are not a warrior,' he finally said.

'You don't like my poem?' asked Izzi.

'A warrior always knows precisely where death sits. If he doesn't, he is no warrior.'

'I will revise it then,' said Izzi.

'I doubt you will live that long,' the leader said, poking gloomily at the fire with a piece of wood.

'I work fast,' said Izzi.

'Every man is like this stick of kindling,' the tall samurai went on, casting it with a precise flip into the fire. 'The question is not when we're going to be destroyed, but with what kind of fire and light we will burn.'

No one spoke. Then he looked up at Oboko.

'You are a poet too?' he asked.

'Yes.'

'Write me a poem. About love.'

'I know nothing about love.'

'About women then. Call it what you will.'

'Izzi has many poems about love. He ...'

'Recite me a poem about women.'

'I feel I have not written ...'

When Oboko saw the samurai's huge right hand grip again the hilt of his short sword he drew his feet in sharply.

'About women?' he quickly asked.

'Yes.'

'My poems are very short.'

'Good. Already you are superior to Izzi.'

Oboko sat up straighter and drew his feet in even closer to his body. He cleared his throat. He looked steadily into the samurai's eyes and then recited:

> The old peasant woman hauls the two buckets
> Up the steep slope. 'Ah,' she remembers,
> 'How Kyno could fuck.'

There was another silence and then the leader began to laugh, deeply and easily, and Izzi and the two other samurai joined him. For perhaps ten seconds the sound of laughter filled the great old hall. Then the tall samurai stopped laughing and so did the others.

'Very fine. Now a poem about a court lady.'

'I have not written one about ...'

The leader's right hand moved half an inch and Oboko felt his right toes twitch.

'It would be nice if you made one up right now,' said the leader.

Oboko hesitated and looked into the fire. When he finally spoke his lines, he didn't know what they were going to be until he heard them himself:

> A beautiful lady sings in the night:
> Hear the heartbeat
> Of the men.

Everyone was silent for a moment, until the tall samurai, looking coldly at Oboko, said:

'Sings ...?'

'Wunnerful. Wunnerful stuff,' said Izzi, holding up his cup of saki. 'With such as this I can die in peace. Why ...'

'Let us hear another poem on the beautiful lady.'

'But ...' Oboko began, '... of course.' He looked down into the dark liquid in his own cup and intoned the lines he didn't know until his own voice spoke them:

> They came to the temple;
> She wasn't there.
> Only two poets
> And their fire.

Another long silence followed until the leader said with sudden vehemence:

'Poets! Fucking poets! What do you know about women? What do you know about Lady Arishi?'

'Nothing,' said Oboko.

'Everything,' said Izzi, 'about women. Not so much about Lady Arishi. In Kyoto they say she's the most beautiful and brilliant woman in Samika. And a marvellous slut.'

The leader's hand was on his great sword seemingly at the same instant that the word 'slut' impinged upon the air, but he didn't draw it from the scabbard.

'You are right in all respects,' he finally said.

'She apparently likes solitude in the snow too,' said Oboko.

'She flees from her fate,' the tall samurai said gravely. 'But she carries death on her back as certainly as I carry this sword.'

'Death for being beautiful and brilliant?' asked Oboko.

'Death for being a slut,' snapped the leader. 'She forgot that the wife of Lord Arishi is the wife of Lord Arishi and not a courtesan or geisha or court poet.'

Oboko wanted to ask more but decided to do so by saying nothing. He noticed that the tall samurai's face showed a tension not there before.

'Unfortunately, my Lady Arishi aspired beyond her place. She received the compliments of a nobleman of the court with behaviour unacceptable to Lord Arishi.'

'And now,' Izzi said, yawning, 'Lord Arishi is sweeping to his revenge with his three best warriors?'

'Yes,' the tall one replied. 'With his three best warriors.'

'A tragic hero,' said Izzi brightening. 'I'm to be the court poet of a tragic hero, of a giant among men. I must write a poem about Lord Arishi's greatness before I arrive there. Before I meet him and become disillusioned.'

'You will not be disillusioned,' said the young samurai.

'And you, captain,' asked Oboko. 'What do you think of your Lord?'

'He is Lord Arishi. He commands, I obey. For me, all his thoughts and actions are correct.'

'Including that you kill his wife?'

'Especially that I kill his wife.'

Seven

Twenty minutes later, Izzi, sprawled supine on the floor, seemed thoroughly drunk, although Oboko doubted it. The tall leader had drunk steadily all that time too, but when he rose to go out into the night with the young samurai to 'look around', he seemed as sober as when he arrived. The third warrior, old and wizened, remained behind, seated erect at the side of Oboko; he too had drunk too much, but acted more drunken than Oboko believed he was. When the door had slammed shut behind the two others, Oboko and the old man turned to search each other's faces casually.

'Your captain seems to like poetry,' Oboko said.

'He is a connoisseur of all the arts.'

'Including killing?'

The old man shrugged.

'It is our job.'

'And this woman that you seek—Lady Arishi—do you look forward to killing her?'

'It is our job.'

'She is beautiful?'

The old one stiffened slightly. When he relaxed he made a kind of snorting sound.

'She is only one,' he said.

'Pardon?'

'Other women are beautiful,' he said. 'When you see Lady Arishi, she is with you for the rest of your life.'

'I see,' Oboko said quietly. 'And was she unfaithful to Lord Arishi?'

A second time the old one stiffened and looked intently at Oboko.

'Probably,' he finally said, examining Oboko. 'She's a woman.'

'I see.'

'No man who sees her, but wants her.'

'And . . .?'

'She's a woman.'

'I see.'

'She could have any man she wanted,' he said, watching Oboko. 'Therefore, undoubtedly, she had plenty.'

'Plenty . . .' Oboko echoed.

'A different nobleman, jester, servant, stranger, having her every night for a year,' the old man went on. 'Limp cocks throughout the land.'

Oboko, pale, sweating, said nothing. He sensed that for some reason the old man was trying to provoke him. The two men stared at each other.

'Her husband was a patient man,' he finally said. 'Very patient. Now, however, he will kill her.'

Oboko looked into the fire.

'Except that most probably she is already dead in the snow.'

'Most probably,' echoed the old man, watching Oboko carefully.

When the tall samurai and his young follower returned, the younger one brought several candles which he lit and placed around the room to supplement the increasingly bright moonlight. When the two men took without comment their positions near the fire opposite Oboko, Izzi stirred, yawned, and sat up.

'Dozed off a bit, I guess,' he said to the leader. 'Incredible stuff you brought.'

'You like our saki?'

'I'll never touch anything else.'

'And you, Oboko?'

'It's very good.'

'And where are you journeying this lovely spring?'

The tall leader was smiling at Oboko pleasantly.

'To the monastery at Nuni Bay.'

'Ah, you are a disciple of Master Eno?'

'Yes.'

'Tell us some stories about him.'

'I'd rather not,' said Oboko.

'You're being stuffy. He's a friend of ... mine,' the tall samurai said.

'Ahhh?'

'I studied with him for three months once.'

'I see.'

The tall samurai, eyes crinkling in good humour, went on:

'One day I went to his door to see him at the accustomed time and knocked. His voice asked: "Who is there?"

'"It is ... I," I answered.

'"There's no room in here for both me and you," Master Eno's voice replied and the door remained shut.'

He was looking at Oboko sternly now as a master might at a disciple. The old man beside him was smiling.

'I went away confused by the exchange,' the leader went on, 'and for several days I spent all my hours meditating upon it. After a week I returned again for the first time to Master Eno's door and knocked.

'His voice from within asked: "Who is there?"

'I said loudly, "It is you."

'The door was opened and I entered.'

Oboko smiled at this well-known parable and, still smiling, looked into the fire.

'So that is what happened?' he said slowly.

'Yes.'

'Because I was standing in the hallway when you gave that second answer,' Oboko went on, creating a parable of his own, 'and, having given it, were admitted. So a few days later I went up to his door and knocked.

'"Who is there?" came Master Eno's voice from within.

'"It is *you*!" I answered loudly.

'"In that case you're already inside," said his voice from within and the door remained shut.'

Except for Izzi, who seemed to be dozing, everyone laughed loudly at Oboko's story. The leader of the samurai, holding an almost empty wine-skin in his lap, seemed to examine Oboko with new respect.

'The man who can play the fool, knowing it,' he said to Oboko, 'may be upon the Path.' He was looking at Oboko with his black eyebrows raised, as if asking a question.

Oboko hesitated.

'Ah, how sad,' commented the leader. 'But you'll stick to it?'

'Yes.'

'Tell me, what is the meaning of Boddhidharma's coming to the west?'

'It was a mistake,' Oboko replied.

The three samurai laughed again.

'Very good, young man,' the leader went on. 'And what is the essence of Buddhism?'

Oboko impulsively reached out his hand and stuck it into the fire. For the few seconds he held it there the three watched him intently. When he'd withdrawn it—the pain was great—they all released their breaths at once.

'You are young,' the tall samurai said. 'Your Buddhism is not dead, as it is with so many, but it is young.'

'And what is the sound of one hand clapping?' Oboko asked him in turn.

'Not much,' answered the other, smiling, as his companions and now Izzi laughed. 'How can you make your mind absolutely pure?' he asked Oboko in return.

'It is easy,' Oboko said.

'How?'

'I think always of dung,' Oboko replied gravely. As the leader smiled, Oboko went on: 'And how do you distinguish between the *maya* of illusion and the *prajna* of truth?'

The tall samurai looked evenly at Oboko for a long moment.

'Illusion is whatever I am thinking,' he finally said, smiling, '*prajna* is the rest.'

The old man to his leader's left emitted a deep-throated laugh.

'And what is the distinction,' the tall one continued, 'between *samsara* and *nirvana*?'

'I do not know,' replied Oboko. 'I have never known *nirvana*.'

'Too bad,' the other replied coldly. 'Having once known *nirvana* you would then, like me, be able to experience the full misery of *samsara*.'

Oboko didn't reply and for several seconds they all looked silently into the fire, Izzi and Oboko being forced to cough loudly when a soft downdraft from the open window puffed smoke sideways over them.

'Great gobs of Buddha,' Izzi spluttered after he'd stopped coughing. 'The wind's punishing us for all this nonsense you've been talking.'

'It only seems nonsense to the unenlightened,' the tall samurai said coldly.

'That must be it,' Izzi said, yawning, and sitting up. 'I studied with six masters over twenty years and only got one insight worth it all.'

Everyone turned to look at Izzi, who, face flushed, eyes half-open, his upper body swaying gently, didn't go on.

'And what is that single insight?' asked the old man with the wrinkled face, leaning forward.

Izzi hiccoughed and groped briefly with his left hand for the wine-skin which lay just beyond his grasp.

'Unfortunately,' he said, 'I've forgotten it.'

The three samurai frowned; Oboko smiled fully.

'But I'll tell you one thing,' Izzi went on, giving up on the wine-skin and scratching his beard. 'All that time I made the mistake of seeing myself as a Buddha living in a world filled with madmen, but now, I see that I'm a—I don't know what—living in a world filled with genuine Buddhas, most of them,' he concluded looking through half-closed eyes at the tall samurai, 'carefully and fully disguised as madmen.'

The tall samurai simply looked back without expression into Izzi's red eyes.

'Great Buddha,' Izzi exploded, shaking his head. 'I've got to have a piss.'

This time the samurai leader smiled.

'Fill our jugs with snow,' he said to the old man to his left. 'It's time for bed.'

The old man arose and moved away to the horses and began to open a bag for the jugs. Izzi, stretching and yawning, shuffled over to the wall near the horses to urinate. Oboko smiled into the fire for a while and then turned back to the tall samurai. He felt the wind swirl in along the floor as the door at the end of the room was opened, and cease swirling as the old man in leaving closed it behind him.

'And what is the Tao, the Way?' Oboko asked the leader.

As Oboko looked to him for the answer, he saw the man's handsome face rise to look past Oboko at something behind him. As it did it was slowly transformed into a look so strange, so agonized, so terrible, that Oboko knew, even as he swung his head quickly to look behind him, that in the hallway stood Matari. In the flickering candlelight, her white gown glimmering, she stood there, silent, her eyes wide with fear.

Slowly, without seeming to move a limb, the tall samurai rose to his feet. His expression was still so strange and tormented that Oboko could not label it. The man and the woman stood staring at each other as if each had been resurrected from the dead. Finally, the man spoke.

'My wife,' he said, and his face organized itself into impassivity.

'My Lord ... Arishi,' Matari replied, but in her face was still fear. Oboko, stunned, slowly absorbing the exchange he'd just heard, looked back at the tall samurai—Lord Arishi—and understood the expression he'd seen.

'I have come to kill you,' Lord Arishi said in a low voice.

Matari stared back at him, her face now slightly controlled, but her body visibly trembling. She glanced once, lost and afraid, at Oboko, then back to her husband, who, slowly, with the effortless grace with which he seemed to do all things, drew from his scabbard his great sword. The sound of its unsheathing echoed through the silent room.

Oboko and the young samurai—as if they were linked by common puppet strings—sprang to their feet and drew their long swords at the same instant. From off near the animals came Izzi's hoarse voice.

'Don't be a fool, 'Boko! Put your sword away. We've nothing to do with this.'

Lord Arishi didn't deign to look at either Oboko or Izzi, but remained facing his wife. Although his features were controlled, sweat glistened in the light of the fire, candles, and moon.

'Matari must die,' he said, again in a low voice.

'No,' Oboko said, 'she must not die.' He was crouched with his back to the wall, trying to watch both the young samurai and Lord Arishi at once. He too was trembling.

'You are young, and a fool,' Lord Arishi said, still looking only at his wife. 'Sheath your sword and leave.'

'Leave, Oboko,' said Matari softly.

Oboko looked at the pale motionless figure of Matari, white against the black hallway; at Lord Arishi, immense and impassive facing her; at the young samurai crouching opposite him; and at Izzi, swaying in the corner by the horses.

'I am young and a fool,' said Oboko quietly. He didn't move.

With a slow dreamlike motion that seemed to go on forever, Lord Arishi's head and eyes turned to his left to look at Oboko.

'You shall have your *nirvana*,' he said.

Oboko's whole body braced for the gesture from Lord

Arishi which would signal the explosion of fury of either the young samurai or of the lord himself.

'No ... Oboko ... please,' came Matari's soft voice.

Lord Arishi's face reddened, and as Oboko crouched yet lower to receive the onslaught, there was a sudden shriek from a horse, and all three men turned to see Izzi, sword in hand, astride the black stallion, wheeling and thundering across the thirty feet of stone towards Lord Arishi.

In a split second Oboko's body acted before his mind could think, his sword slashing out and ripping into the sword arm of the young samurai at the same time as he himself fell away from the sweep of Lord Arishi's long sword, the end of whose blade sliced through his cape, jacket and chest in a swift unbroken line, the pain sharp and clean, the blood warm and wet beneath his clothing. Oboko was on the ground, the young samurai groaning, grasping his arm and rolling away from him. Lord Arishi had turned to take the rush of Izzi on the horse, and Oboko saw him leap to one side and strike a tremendous blow at Izzi, smashing his sword out of his hand, cutting him and knocking him from the plunging horse.

Oboko was on his feet, and even as his sword seemed to be falling on the unseeing back of Lord Arishi, the lord was turning away to parry the blow, Matari shouting a single ambiguous 'No!' the two swords clanging together, pain ripping through Oboko's wrist. He staggered backwards, twisting his sword to stop the seemingly instantaneous return sweep of Arishi's long blade, Oboko's sword falling away from his hand as if by witchcraft.

Lord Arishi wheeled again but this time too late to stop Izzi's bull-like body from smashing into his thighs, toppling him backwards towards the stunned and terrified Oboko. When Lord Arishi rolled away from Izzi and raised his sword, Oboko's foot smashed into his arm, knocking the sword to the ground. Izzi was now struggling with the young samurai, and even as Oboko leaped on to Lord Arishi he saw the door opening and the old man rushing sword in hand, towards them.

Oboko screamed in rage and terror and swung his fist at Lord Arishi's face, feeling as he did his body being flung by Arishi upwards head over heels past the lord's head. Like a circus performer he rolled quickly two or three times to the spot where the young samurai had left his sword. He scrambled to his feet just in time to meet the first thrust of the old samurai, to parry and strike, strike and parry, Matari white and motionless in the candlelight to his left.

The old samurai fell from a thrust of Oboko's sword in his stomach, a thrust which seemed as much the chance of witchcraft as had been his own disarming by Lord Arishi. When he turned he saw Izzi being slammed against the wall by a brutal swing of Arishi's fist, and sliding in a heap to the floor. Lord Arishi swung around and strode two paces towards Oboko before he saw the blood-red sword. He stopped.

Lord Arishi was two steps from Oboko, but three steps from the nearest sword abandoned on the floor. Behind him, Izzi groaned and began to shake his head. His old samurai lay silent and bleeding just to the right of Oboko; the young one was gasping and writhing a few feet away. Alone and mute in the entrance to the hallway stood Matari. Lord Arishi and Oboko were crouched facing each other, Arishi unarmed.

'No ...' Matari said softly.

Oboko was bent, sweating, no longer frightened, but his eyes glued to Lord Arishi.

'Don't move,' Oboko whispered.

Lord Arishi didn't move. Izzi had risen to his knees, still shaking his head.

'Don't move,' he hissed again. He didn't want to kill Lord Arishi, but knew that if the man ever held a sword in his hand again, death would follow. He had disarmed both Oboko and Izzi with one sword swing each, and flattened Izzi with a single blow of his fist.

Izzi was on his feet, his eyes beginning to focus. When he began to grasp the situation he reached into his belt and drew out his short sword. He moved slowly towards Lord Arishi's back.

Oboko saw, but didn't quite grasp the meaning. Izzi's hand was raised a scant three feet from Arishi's back when Oboko's stare, Matari's scream, and Lord Arishi's swift duck and swing of his arm all seemed to occur at once. Arishi's blow smashed into Izzi's belly doubling him up and knocking him to his knees. Arishi completed a gymnastic roll and was on his feet again, but Oboko had leaped there too and stood facing him, still only two strides away.

Izzi was struggling to his feet yet a third time, like some comic enduring a series of pratfalls, and when he'd done so he looked bewilderingly around him until he relocated Lord Arishi. His eyes brightened in anger. As Oboko saw him start to move towards Arishi, he said sharply:

'No, Izzi, no. He's unarmed. We can't kill him.'

'Unarmed!' Izzi said. 'That bastard is never unarmed.'

'We can't kill him,' Oboko said again, still crouched and intent on Arishi, who, breathing heavily, straightened himself and seemed at last to relax.

''Boko, 'Boko, we must!' Izzi exclaimed, now beside his friend. 'As long as he's alive, we're as good as dead.'

'We can't kill him unless he resists,' Oboko hissed through clenched teeth.

Izzi looked at Oboko and began to laugh. His laughter had a strange hysterical quality in the moonlit room with the dying men.

'Great belly of Buddha,' Izzi said, shaking his head. 'Are you going through the rest of your life twisted up like that?'

'Get some rope and tie him,' Oboko said. 'We'll take him as hostage.'

Izzi looked at the tall, serene Lord Arishi and then at Oboko, small and crouched.

'Since when do sheep take lions hostage?' he asked. 'We can't kill him.'

There the four stood: Arishi erect and smiling; Izzi slumped and bloody, shaking his head; Oboko, body and teeth clenched; Matari alone behind them.

'I am sorry, dear Matari,' Lord Arishi now said to her. 'But I have been delayed.'

Matari moved. Slowly she glided from her position near the hallway, past the body of the old samurai, past Oboko and Izzi to a spot beside the silent body of the young samurai a few yards from Lord Arishi. She looked at her husband for a long time, her eyes beginning to glisten with tears.

'Why can't you let me go?' she finally cried to him.

Lord Arishi gazed back at her coldly.

'I have judged,' he replied.

'I have lied to you and asked to leave,' she went on, her voice urgent. 'Why must you try to kill me?'

'I have *vowed* to kill you,' Lord Arishi answered, his face still impassive and his breathing becoming easier. He seemed to feel the vow was sufficient answer.

'Permit us to leave this temple in peace,' she pleaded, 'I to the south, you back to Samika.'

The answer when it came from him, standing as erect and motionless as a statue, seemed inevitable.

'I have vowed,' he said.

Matari stopped speaking. She continued to look at Lord Arishi with her chin slightly forward and her body tensed as if it strained to influence him with its set. Then her shoulders abruptly relaxed. After almost half a minute she turned to Oboko.

'Kill him,' she said.

The room was absolutely silent. The young samurai no longer breathed, and only a gentle wind in the fir trees outside provided any sound.

'Kill him,' she said again softly, her moist eyes pleading now with Oboko from her tormented face.

'Kill him,' said Izzi, himself joining Oboko in a crouch, his knife in hand.

'We cannot kill him,' Oboko said. 'Get a rope.'

Izzi straightened. Lord Arishi turned to look at his wife.

'Thank you, Matari,' he said, 'for your confidence in me.'

Matari was still looking at Oboko.

'If you don't kill him . . .' her voice trailed off.

'If you don't kill me, Oboko, then Matari will die.'

'No one should die,' Oboko said.

Izzi moved off to the saddlebags in the far corner and found rope. Returning, he moved, knife in hand, up behind Lord Arishi.

'Put your arms behind your back,' Oboko said.

Lord Arishi put his arms behind his back, and Izzi, with the knife now between his teeth, began to tie his hands.

'I don't want to discourage you,' Lord Arishi said. 'But you might want to know that as soon as the snow stops completely—as it has now apparently—a patrol of my finest horsemen will be on its way up after us.'

Izzi finished binding the arms and moved away from Lord Arishi, holding the end of the rope he'd used.

'Now,' said Oboko, straightening up from his crouch for the first time in minutes, 'you are our hostage.'

Lord Arishi laughed.

'You are a fool,' he said. 'You should kill me.'

'You are our hostage,' Oboko said again.

Lord Arishi looked slowly from Oboko to Matari and then back to Oboko.

'And you,' he said quietly, 'my prisoners.'

Part Two

The Hunt

The black hare leaps, and flees
My horse's heavy rush,
Darts and swerves
My arrow's horizontal slice,
Runs and hides, black
To the earth's blackness,
And I joy.
I joy in each leap,
Each swerve,
Each hiding,
As I shall joy, in the end,
In holding aloft,
Lifeless,
The hare.

attributed to Lord Arishi

Eight

As their three horses carried them at a slow walk through the deep drifts of snow back up towards the Kybo pass, the half moon hung over their heads like a silver guillotine. Since leaving two hours before dawn they had paused only once, on a rise a few hundred yards from the temple, to see below them on the trail winding up from Samika a long line of tiny lights: Lord Arishi's horsemen in pursuit. How far away they yet were, it was impossible to tell.

Oboko and Matari, being the smallest, rode together on the leading horse, the black stallion. Lord Arishi, his hands now bound together in front of him to the reins, and each foot tied to a stirrup, followed next on the white mare. At the rear on the grey gelding—which was attached to Arishi's mare—rode Izzi, cursing at the slowness of Oboko's pace and continually glancing behind him at the vast expanses of moonlit snow which would all too soon be filled with their pursuers.

Before leaving the temple Oboko and Izzi had cleaned, staunched and bound their wounds. Lord Arishi's sword had cut a clean six inch line an inch deep just beneath the left side of Oboko's rib cage. He cleaned it with one of his cotton shirts, rubbed on to and around it a herb ointment he always carried with him and then used the same shirt tied around his middle to press against the wound a clean cotton scarf which Matari brought him. Izzi's wounds were mostly a collection of bumps and bruises which made him feel, he said, as if all the blows he'd suffered previously in his life had suddenly blossomed at once.

Matari had administered as best she could to the wounds of the old samurai. Although Oboko's sword thrust had gone all the way through his abdomen to emerge from his back beneath the rib cage, the old man still lived and seemed able to drink water without pain. As Matari bent over the old man, Oboko saw him look at her with an expression not of anger or hatred for what had passed, but of warmth and pity.

'Live, old one,' Matari whispered, and the old man held her eyes in his for a moment and then looked away.

'Some are meant to live, some die,' he said. He didn't look at her again.

After leaving him next to a warm fire with enough water, fruit and rice cake to last a day, and after Matari had collected carefully into one bag the clothing and jewellery she'd brought with her, they had to help Izzi bury the young samurai. But outside in the moonlight where Lord Arishi was kneeling silently beside the peaceful, seemingly unmarked body of the young man, Izzi suggested that if they left the body unburied, Arishi's horsemen would be forced to take care of it before continuing the chase. When Lord Arishi rose from his young follower's body, Oboko saw on his face the same strange, tormented look he'd showed when he'd first seen Matari. When they rode away, they left before the door of the old temple, as the only ostensible evidence that they had visited, the young warrior's dead body.

Through the bright night silently they pushed southwards, following not so much anything which could be called a trail as the indentation in the terrain. Rocks, boulders, and occasional fir trees loomed up to the left and right of them like silent mourners watching the riders, hunched down against the wind, moving along in single file like prisoners tied to one another on a death march.

An hour after the sun slid white and cold over the eastern ridge of the world, they reached the high point of the northern end of the pass and began the long sloping journey across the high, uneven plateau to the southern end, which would lead, at last, downwards to the sea. Their destination was the port city of Lissa, where Matari would be safe. It would normally have been a long day's ride at full gallop; through the deep snow at their crawl it meant at least two. Although Lord Arishi made no effort to delay them, the black stallion, with its two riders, was awkward and slow moving. It seemed that at least once each hour he would stumble into a drift and, while Lord Arishi cursed sullenly—as if at their incompetence—they would have to wait for Oboko and Matari to dismount and lead the horse to a better footing.

After their horse stumbled a third time, Matari quietly suggested that Oboko ride forward and she would sit behind him. When she placed her arms around his waist and buried her hands under his cloak, Oboko was acutely conscious of their pressure, but then, as she held him thus for warmth and balance against a fall, he relaxed into forgetting their existence.

Later, the legs of the black stallion plunged once more into a sudden softness in the snow, and the two riders fell head-first over the horse's head. This time Matari rolled over laughing, her long black hair falling free from her scarf and lying like a pool of spilled ink on the snow. Oboko too smiled happily until he looked up and saw above, hands tied before him, Lord Arishi, staring down upon them without expression.

All through the bright morning they rode south in silence, their path winding through gorges and along ridges and past rock formations sculpted in lovely forms by the drifted snow, their path an intricate design to the south, a design which Oboko and Izzi hoped they were guessing correctly. Once, they dead-ended at a cliff-face and had to retrace their way, Lord Arishi again wild-eyed and cursing their stupidity. Twice during the day they saw their pursuers. Glancing back just before noon they saw horsemen coming through the high point of the pass far behind them. They could now gauge that they were about three hours away. Two hours later Oboko caught a brief glimpse of two riders disappearing behind a ridge. Closer.

When they occasionally stopped to rest or to feed the horses, all four of them seemed numb. Oboko didn't know whether it was lack of sleep, exhaustion from their hours on horseback, or the dazed feeling that events had long ago begun to move too swiftly for even the wisest man to know how to avoid catastrophe. Each brief stop would pass in silence until, one by one, without words, they would remount and ride on. Twice Izzi handed to Oboko the rope connected to Lord Arishi's horse and forced his gelding off on a fork to try to create a false trail to delay the pursuing samurai, but after the second attempt he decided that he was tiring himself more than he would his pursuers. In the afternoon, clouds began rolling in off the distant sea; within two hours it had clouded over so completely that they knew that the blackness of the night would make movement for them, without light of any kind, so slow and tortuous as to be impossible. The samurai, with torches and fuel, could still ride.

An hour before sunset they came to a high point. The three horses came to a stop abreast of each other, breathing heavily, and their riders all looked off towards the south, across the snow-blanketed high-ground dotted here and there with protruding wind swept rocks, past a single large, jutting pinnacle, to the distant dim horizon beyond which lay, gods willing, the already green valleys of Lissa, and the sea.

'In daylight,' said Oboko in a subdued voice, 'when we're once below the snowline it's only an eight hour ride to Lissa.'

Izzi was taking a long swallow from his wine-skin and looking off to the left.

'With arrows in your back it's slower,' Lord Arishi said; his horse was between the two others, but he looked stonily forward.

Izzi lowered the wine-skin to his side, leaned forward in

his saddle and looked across Lord Arishi's horse to Oboko and Matari.

'We'll never have a better spot to see those dwarfs chasing us than from up there,' he said, and pointed to a high point thirty yards off from their trail to the left. 'We can see behind us for at least a mile,' he went on, 'and if they ride tonight, they'll have to use torches.'

'Do you plan to serve them dinner?' Lord Arishi asked. He hadn't bothered to turn in his saddle.

Izzi took another long drink of the wine.

'No,' he said. 'If they're as bad as you, they probably all drink too much.'

Lord Arishi didn't smile.

'Then how do you propose to stop them from coming uninvited?' he asked.

'We'll cover over our trail up to the camp,' said Oboko, 'and create a false trail continuing on from where we are here.'

'We've still got almost an hour before dark,' said Izzi, now squinting at the distant horizon in front of them. 'I'll stamp out a path with the grey out to that pinnacle there, create a few offshoots, and then ride back ...'

'No,' Matari interrupted softly from behind Oboko. 'We will be cut off. You should make a circle.'

'Why a circle?' Izzi asked.

'We don't want them to stop for the night to the south of us,' Matari answered.

'But what circle?' Oboko asked, turning his head slightly to see Matari peering past his shoulder.

'She means,' said Lord Arishi irritably, 'that you ought to make your false trail go in a half-moon out to the right from here, arc towards the pinnacle, pass it from right to left as we see it from here, then continue circling left to return to the camp you're going to make, from ... over there.' He pointed now forward and to the left.

'Around on this side,' said Matari softly, pointing past Oboko's left shoulder to the left, 'near the end of your circle, you should dismount and try to cover over thirty or forty feet of your path. If you do it right they may think they have been led into a deadend.'

Oboko and Izzi were silent for a moment absorbing what had been said.

'I didn't know Lady Arishi was a samurai,' Izzi said after a while, taking another drink and smiling.

'My husband ...' Matari began and then was silent.

Oboko, feeling the tension of the silence which followed, leaned towards Izzi.

'Do you want me to do it?' he asked.

Izzi repacked the wine-skin in the saddlebag, glanced briefly at Oboko, then set his horse slowly walking forward.

'No thanks, 'Boko,' he said without looking back. 'I'll ride, and you can let the Arishis show you how to make camp.' Oboko thought he heard Izzi laugh.

Oboko signalled Lord Arishi to lead the way off their trail up the incline to the small ridge behind which they would camp. They climbed awkwardly up the thirty yards of uneven hillside, then more easily on level ground between two huge boulders, emerging into a partially enclosed circle of large rocks.

Matari and Oboko dismounted. While Matari led the black stallion off to tether it to a scrub pine growing out of one of the boulders, Oboko moved to untie Lord Arishi's feet from his stirrups. When both feet were freed, Oboko drew his sword and asked Lord Arishi to dismount. Matari, returning, then untied the rope which bound her husband to the reins of his horse, as she did so keeping her eyes rigidly on her task. She did not look at Lord Arishi, whose hands, at Oboko's orders, were left tied in front of him.

'We'll now have to tie you with your back against that tree,' Oboko said to him, and indicated another scrub pine off to his right.

Lord Arishi stood quietly where he had dismounted.

'It seems,' he said, 'that I am doomed to spend an

infinite amount of time staring, hands tied, at the point of your sword.'

'It's a tribute to your skills,' Oboko replied quietly, and then asked Matari to go back to the stallion and bring more rope.

'Still, couldn't you admire me more comfortably?' Lord Arishi asked.

'You'll be bound to that tree and your feet tied. Otherwise we'll do what we can to make you comfortable.'

Lord Arishi's mocking face turned cold.

'I will not be humiliated,' he said. He was pale. He still hadn't moved.

'We're not letting you escape,' answered Oboko. 'You will be tied.'

'No,' said Lord Arishi. 'No more. Not in front of ... *her*,' he added softly, moving his head slightly to the right.

'You'll have to do what my sword commands.'

'No,' he said firmly, almost relaxed. 'No. I can die.'

Oboko stared at him.

'Rather than be bound?' Oboko asked doubtfully.

'I will not live as a slave.'

Oboko stared at him.

'Move over to that tree,' he said in a firm voice.

'No,' Lord Arishi replied quietly. 'Undo these binds.'

Oboko, crouched now, sword ready, waited. Matari returned with the additional rope.

'What ... what is happening?' she asked.

'Oboko is getting ready to untie my hands,' said Lord Arishi, 'or kill me. He hasn't decided which.'

'Untie you!'

'Yes. I feel like building a snowman.'

'Oboko ...' said Matari uncertainly.

'I can release you,' Oboko said to Lord Arishi slowly, 'if you give me your word to try neither to escape nor to harm any of the three of us.'

'Ahhh,' said Lord Arishi, 'and why should I give you such a depressing promise?'

'If you don't,' Oboko replied, wondering indeed what he could possibly do, 'or don't do as I command, then ... I shall have to kill you.'

'Ah, but I thought you were against killing.'

Oboko didn't answer. He remained crouched in his set position conscious of Matari standing a few feet to his left looking uncertainly from the one man to the other. Could he kill an unarmed Lord Arishi? In front of Matari? It was absurd, Oboko felt absurd, they all suddenly seemed absurd, like characters in some farce written by ... a court poet.

'Move to that tree,' Oboko said.

Lord Arishi, still standing erect and unmoving where he had first dismounted, smiled fully.

'You are young, Oboko, and a fool,' he said. 'How did you ever get yourself into this mess?'

'I'm young,' Oboko said, 'and a fool. Move to that tree.'

'Oboko—' Matari began.

'And my word?' Lord Arishi interrupted. 'You will accept only my *word* that I won't try to escape or to harm you?'

Oboko looked at him carefully and did not answer. His instinctive answer was 'no'.

'Well, wife,' Lord Arishi said to Matari, his eyes narrow and mocking. 'Tell him. Advise him. Should he trust my word?'

Oboko glanced at Matari who turned slowly away from her husband until her back was to him. Looking off past Oboko into the distance she said softly:

'Yes.'

Oboko remained uncertain.

'If he gives his word,' Matari went on, 'hell will melt before he breaks it.'

'How interesting!' exclaimed Lord Arishi. 'A *man's* word may be trusted.'

'Let me hear your promise,' said Oboko.

Lord Arishi replied with a sardonic grin:

'I, Lord Arishi, do unenthusiastically give my unbreakable word that, unbound and unwatched, I shall neither try to escape nor try to harm anyone, this vow to hold until ... until we are touched by the white cherry blossoms of spring!' He beamed exaggeratedly as if being witty.

Oboko looked at Lord Arishi's out of character grin, glanced at Matari—who still looked past him without expression—and then, rising from his crouch, sheathed his sword. He went forward and began to untie Lord Arishi's hands. When they were free, he turned his back on Lord Arishi, took the extra rope which Matari had brought, and walked slowly towards the black stallion. Needles danced down his back; his whole body was sweating. Over his shoulder he said to either of them:

'There's food for the horses in that right saddlebag.'

'Get me a drink,' he heard Lord Arishi say to Matari, but, when he finally reached the black stallion and was able to sneak a glance back, he saw her still standing with her back to her husband. Without replying to him she began slowly to walk across the snow to Oboko. Arishi, rubbing his wrists, looked at her, then spat into the trampled snow where she'd stood. Giving Oboko a brief cold stare, he then turned to his horse and began to unpack.

Nine

In the next ten minutes Oboko and Matari worked in silence tethering the two horses, feeding them, and unpacking food, blankets, and the firewood they'd brought from the temple. The thick layer of clouds stretching from horizon to horizon prevented him from knowing whether the sun had actually set, but already when he looked southwards now, Oboko could no longer see the pinnacle past which Izzi was to ride. Lord Arishi began to build a fire against a large boulder, which, with the wind still blowing warm from the south, would send the smoke away from the sleeping area. When Oboko told Matari that he had to go back to disguise their departure from the main trail, she insisted that she follow.

Together they trudged through the snow between the two big boulders, beside one of which Lord Arishi, his back turned, was patiently planting twigs and kindling, and down the short hillside to the main trail. It seemed to Oboko that the snow was too much trampled at the intersection, but he was uncertain what to do about it. Matari stood a few feet away looking first at the snow around their feet and then back northwards.

'We might as well leave this,' Oboko said aloud. 'It makes it look as if we'd stopped here before going on.' He moved off the trail on to the crunched snow which led up to their camp. Matari followed. As Oboko turned right at the edge of the main trail to begin to cover over their path to the camp she said:

'Why don't we leave five or ten feet disturbed here to the left? It would look more natural.'

Thinking of Izzi's parting words, Oboko smiled, first to himself, then to Matari.

'Yes,' he said, and together they moved ten more feet away from the trail and there began filling in the path. They worked slowly, scooping up handfuls of snow or pushing large areas of it, then sculpting the top surface to match the flow of snow on either side. Since the flakes were soft and powdery, it was easy to create a surface quite close to what must have been there before their two horses had pushed through. Oboko, his hands cold but his body warm from the exacting work, decided they would have to cover over only the first thirty or forty feet of the one hundred feet of disturbed snow leading to their camp since, in the black of the approaching night, the light of torches would carry no further. Also, it seemed unlikely that the pursuing samurai, after looking mile after mile for exactly this sort of camouflaged detour, tired, blinded to the darkness from looking at their torches, would detect whatever small flaws he and Matari might leave.

As he worked beside her in the gathering darkness, the feeling of absurdity which had struck him so forcefully after Lord Arishi had dismounted seemed totally to have disappeared. Sculpting snow over a trampled path with a beautiful and aristocratic lady, whose hand as they worked he sometimes brushed, all to avoid being split open by the sword of some samurai he'd never seen and never hoped to see, struck him, strangely, as natural and delightful. It reminded him vaguely of playing with an older sister when he was a boy. Once or twice he paused to lick at the cold flakes, hold them on his tongue until they'd melted. When he once saw Matari doing the same thing they smiled at each other and then looked away.

When they had finished and returned to their camp it was almost dark. Lord Arishi's fire was burning quietly and he himself seated cross-legged on a blanket drinking saki from a wine-skin. As they walked past him in the gathering dusk and squatted with outstretched hands to warm their frozen fingers, he didn't turn to look at them but continued to stare, icily, into the fire.

Gathering snow into an earthenware teapot, Oboko built a little spot in the firewood for it to sit, while Matari spread a second blanket out on to the packed snow in front of the fire a few feet from her husband. After the water had begun to heat Oboko seated himself on the blanket, cross-legged, and again stretched forth his hands for warmth.

Without a word being spoken by any of them Matari brought and set beside each of the men two large squares of rice cake, now partially frozen, some pieces of dried fish, a small earthenware plate of olives (which she set between them), and a second wine-skin of wine, which she set beside Oboko. After she had finished, she remained standing behind and between them, silent, while they, seated, silent, not touching the food she had brought, stared unflinchingly into the fire.

Oboko began to fear that they might remain thus forever. Seated as he was at one side of their strange tense triangle—it was attaining absurdity again—he could not bring himself to eat without Matari nor yet could he bring himself in front of Lord Arishi to command her to join them before the fire. He felt himself to be at one and the same time Lord Arishi's jailor and his court fool; at the same time Matari's saviour and her obsequious servant. He was immobilized by indecision. Lord Arishi seemed to be determined to ignore her existence and she, for reasons he couldn't grasp, was not joining them uninvited. It was absurd; Oboko felt like screaming.

After what seemed like more than five minutes, Lord Arishi broke the tableau by reaching a hand down, raising a hunk of the rice cake to his mouth and beginning to eat. After chewing noisily on his first bite he turned, at last, to Oboko.

'We have no servant's kitchen,' he commented with an ironical frown.

Oboko immediately stood up, angry, and turned to Matari.

'Please, Matari ... Lady Ari ... Ma ... Lady Arishi,' he began, stammering over her name because her eyes were meeting his with such incredible cold contempt that he felt himself condemned forever to insignificance. 'Pl ... please warm yourself here by the fire and let me bring you food.'

'Bring me some dried fruit first, woman,' Lord Arishi said lazily, beginning to chew again on his rice cake.

'Please sit,' Oboko said to Matari and moved quickly past her to the bare rock where they had unloaded some of their food. After collecting on a single plate the rice, dried fish, and dried apricots and figs, he returned. The two Arishis were as he had left them, silent and unmoved, he looking at the fire, she out northwards into the gathering blackness of the night.

Oboko moved up close to Matari and faced her. He said softly, aware, terrifyingly aware, that Lord Arishi was seated six feet away:

'Please forgive me, Matari, for my rudeness, for *our* rudeness.'

'Where are the figs?' Lord Arishi snapped loudly.

Oboko started to turn to deliver the dried fruit but caught himself and continued to look into Matari's cold eyes. For a moment she held him thus and then her face twisted into pain; she looked away and, face averted, replied simply:

'Let us eat.'

Matari having seated herself between the two men, their meal passed in silence. Once, as the dusk seemed to be melting into total darkness, Oboko rose to leave and stare southwards where Izzi should be soon emerging to rejoin their camp. He shouted once, a brief urgent 'Ho!' but heard no reply. He couldn't see more than thirty feet out into the night.

When they had finished eating, Matari removed the old earthenware teapot from the fire and rose to get three cups from the bag on the bare rock. Returning, she dropped to her knees. As she gracefully began to pour the tea into the cups, Oboko recalled the image of Master Eno pouring tea for his disciples in his *Rokshi* at the monastery at Nuni Bay. There also the ceremony had been done in silence, but there all had been serene, at one with each other. Each disciple recognized the authority of the Master, each aware too of his precise relation with each of the others. One's every act during the tea ceremony was prescribed by tradition; the pouring of the tea, the handing of the cups, the holding of the cup, the first sip, the time spent in the drinking, the placing of the cups on the hard wooden floor upon which the Master and his disciples sat. Every decision having already been made, each act became a work of devotion and of art.

Here, in the darkness, Matari, her white silk gown flickering orange and red, was serving, but here there was no recognized authority, no defined relationships, no prescribed tradition. The silence and stillness and grace of their movements, as Lord Arishi and then he accepted from her trembling hand an earthenware cup, were not the result of inner serenity but of rigid inner control against a chaos as red and unpredictable as the dancing flames on Matari's dress and face.

And when they had all finished drinking the tea and sat each with his tea cup held lightly on his lap looking quietly at the red coals and occasional white tongues of the fire, it seemed to Oboko that perhaps the very act of sharing the tea together had given them at the end the serenity they were supposed to have had in the act itself. He himself, at any rate, felt desperately, determinedly calm. When Lord Arishi cleared his throat Oboko turned to him with polite attention as if they would now begin some fine philosophical after-dinner talk. The small flames of the fire were dappling his usually dark face with flecks of white as he looked up and stared directly for the first time at his wife.

'Well, Matari,' he said. 'I see you have made some new friends.'

Exactly, thought Oboko, exactly.

But Matari didn't reply.

'Izzi was to have been our new court poet,' Lord Arishi went on.

Silence.

'But I'm afraid,' he said, then paused, 'that he's recited the last lines we shall ever be privileged to hear.'

Matari, holding her cup now with both hands tightly against her knees, continued to look only at the red cinders a few feet in front of her.

'He is a great poet,' Oboko said when the lengthening silence had become too great.

Lord Arishi ignored him; he was leaning forward now towards his wife.

'But if he uses his penis as badly as his pen,' he said to her, 'I'm sure you'll agree he is no great loss.'

The chaos could not be controlled. Oboko, surprised, angry, stared coldly at Lord Arishi and said:

'You ... you are losing your dignity.'

'*Am* I?' said Lord Arishi, with an ugly grin. 'Well, that tends to happen to the husband of Matari.'

'I would be pleased if you'd be silent,' said Oboko.

'I gave no vow of silence,' said Lord Arishi.

'I ask, I don't command.'

'You're learning,' Lord Arishi commented and, setting his tea cup near the fire, he reached for the wine-skin and raised it to his lips. When he lowered it after a long swallow, he looked again at Matari.

'And Oboko,' he said, grinning, and Oboko noticed that Matari was trembling, 'while no doubt a better poet than Izzi, would be, I fear, *between* the sheets ...'

Oboko leaped up, hand on sword. Lord Arishi's grinning face, flickering demonically in the firelight, broke into laughter. There was a noise: a horse neighed from the south, and then there was a shout. Oboko turned, shouted back his 'Ho!' and pushed his way through the snow away from the fire.

Within two minutes Izzi was among them, breathing hard, cursing, smiling, and, even before reaching the fire, gulping down huge mouthfuls of the offered wine. Matari, taking the reins of Izzi's exhausted horse, let her eyes meet those of Oboko for only an instant: they said nothing. She led the horse away.

'Great gobs of hell,' Izzi said, shaking his head and crumpling up in a heap in Oboko's place near the fire. 'That ground is shit; great rock turds every ten feet.'

'Did you complete the circle?' Oboko asked, seating himself where Matari had been sitting.

'A circle by a drunken clown, but a circle,' he replied. 'I had to keep doubling back to try to make it seem trampled by three horses. That and those damn rocks ...'

'They won't be fooled,' Lord Arishi said, now leaning back against packed snow pressed to a rock, his eyes closed.

'Maybe not,' said Izzi, 'but they'll have to follow it all out anyway. Maybe I did such a bad job they'll think that it must be a fake fake and thus the real thing.' He smiled brightly and took another healthy swallow from the wine-skin. Lord Arishi opened his eyes for a second as if to consider this subtlety and then closed them again.

'Living Buddha!' Izzi suddenly exclaimed. 'What's Lord Arishi doing untied?'

'He's given his vow not to try to escape or harm us,' Oboko said, handing Izzi some dried fish he himself had left uneaten.

Izzi stuffed his mouth half full with a chunk of it and looked from Oboko to Lord Arishi, who was casually leaning back against the rock holding the second wine-skin.

'And you're still *alive*?' Izzi asked, frowning back at Oboko.

'Apparently,' Oboko answered.

'Where's his great sword?' Izzi asked.

'Still lashed to the black stallion,' said Oboko.

'Well,' said Izzi, beginning to chew, 'now that I think about it, I guess I'll feel safer with Lord Arishi guarding Lord Arishi than I would with only us guarding him.'

Matari came and set food beside Izzi and then announced quietly to Oboko that she was going up to the nearby ridge to watch the trail from the north for a light from their pursuers. Oboko began to insist that he should go, but she cut him short with a 'no', and moved swiftly away.

While Izzi gnawed and chewed and swallowed and spat at the various parts of his meal, Oboko and Lord Arishi sat to his left without speaking. All were exhausted, and Lord Arishi and Izzi, drinking steadily, were soon partly drunk. For ten minutes they sat in complete stillness, the wind having died away to nothing and the only sound being an occasional hiss or snap from the fire. Lord Arishi, eyes again closed, leaned back against his snow-packed boulder, while Izzi stared bleary-eyed into the fire. Oboko had curled up in a huddled heap and began trying to doze. After another ten minutes, Izzi spat once, neatly, into the fire, which swallowed his offering with a hiss.

'I'm out of my mind,' he finally said, breaking the silence. He looked down at Oboko huddled beside him and then over to Lord Arishi leaning against the rock.

'I'm mad.'

Lord Arishi opened his eyes once, closed them; Oboko stirred slightly as if at some minor itch, but said nothing.

'I, Ushiwassa Kuru, Izzi, the poet laureate of the court of Maffli, poet designate of the glorious court of Arishi of Samika, am now, somehow, sitting in the snow, drinking frozen saki, fleeing as fast as my belly will bounce away from my city of triumph, in the company of my master Lord Arishi, who, instead of planning to heap laurels upon my head, is sitting beside me coolly considering which place in my noble body he will plunge his sword.'

'I have already decided,' said Lord Arishi, eyes closed.

'And beside me sits my young friend Oboko, thinking he is courageously saving a lady in distress because of moral principle, when the most innocent Buddhist monk would tell him that he, the poet of the wind, is being helplessly blown hither and yon across the mountains by a single warm, rhythmic breath.'

Oboko shrugged and squirmed; to speak or not to speak: both would miss the truth. He kept his eyes closed.

'And I,' Izzi went on, slowly pouring saki from the wine-skin into his cup, 'world-weary wise man ...' he drank the whole cup in a single long gulp, '... follow.'

The fire hissed and snapped; Lord Arishi shifted an outstretched leg.

'You can leave,' said Oboko, still curled.

'Oh yes, I can leave,' Izzi replied harshly, and he spat into the fire.

'You can leave,' Oboko said again, stirring, 'and you should.'

'Oh yes, I should leave.' Izzi's bleary eyes roamed restlessly to Oboko and then out to the edge of the night. 'And when the tangled spool is at last unwound and you and Matari are well buried, I can gallop back to Samika to take up my position as court poet for Lord Arishi.'

'I would welcome you,' said Lord Arishi, eyes still closed, 'with open dungeon.'

'I'd be the only court poet in our history,' went on Izzi as if he hadn't heard, 'whose first, last, and only line would be ...' (his face broke into a brief self-mocking grin, then reverted to gloom) 'whose first, last and only line would be ... "ouch".' His guttural giggle was so harsh and deep that it sounded as if he were trying hoarsely to clear his throat from an unyielding obstruction.

Lord Arishi sat up and opened his eyes wide. He

looked off to where Matari was keeping watch. Ignoring Izzi he said to Oboko:

'You must know ... that they'll be here within ... the next hour.'

'Perhaps,' said Oboko.

'I'll have to prepare my death poem now,' said Izzi, still staring out into the blackness which surrounded them, 'since it'll be difficult to compose with my body severed from my head.'

'And you still don't know what you'll do?' asked Lord Arishi of Oboko.

Oboko now struggled into a sitting position and held his left hand out close to the dying fire.

'We will always know where they are,' he said, 'but for them we will be the invisible darkness within the darkness.'

'If I shout?'

'Then, at last, we can kill you,' Oboko replied.

'The trouble with death,' Izzi went on aloud to himself, 'is that you spend half a lifetime worrying about him sneaking up on you and then, suddenly, he's sneaked up on you.' He frowned.

Lord Arishi leaned towards the fire.

'And will you fight?'

'When they come, they come,' Oboko said. 'One can't measure the wind until the wind blows.'

'And now that he's sneaked up on me,' said Izzi, still frowning, 'I don't seem to have much to bribe him to go away.'

'But, unfortunately, my men will move in groups. You won't be able to avoid finding yourself trapped.'

'Perhaps,' said Oboko quietly.

'Friendship and honour I could offer him,' brooded Izzi, 'but I have the feeling in this case it's not going to be enough.'

'It seems simplest for you to leave me and Matari here with my word that I won't have you hunted. Otherwise I'll probably have to kill you all.'

'You might.'

'That would be a waste,' said Lord Arishi. 'Poets, even mediocre ones, are always hard to find.'

Matari emerged, standing slightly behind and between Lord Arishi and Oboko who noticed her at the same moment; Izzi was still contemplating his inner vision.

'They're coming,' she announced simply.

Lord Arishi and Oboko glanced at each other.

'A single torch became visible fifteen minutes ago,' she went on quietly. 'None other has appeared. They ... it ... moves very slowly ... towards us.'

'I will take the watch now,' said Oboko, pushing himself quickly to his feet.

'No.'

'You need rest and I ...'

'I don't wish to be ... *here*,' she said, and without another word she again left them.

This time Oboko followed her into the darkness, his hand instinctively falling to the hilt of his sword, although he knew the samurai must still be far away. He lost sight of Matari in the blackness and had to whisper her name once and await her simple 'here' before he was able finally to kneel in the foot deep snow beside where she knelt and look north. Or at least he assumed it was north. There was nothing but blackness on every side.

'The light appears and disappears,' Matari said in a strange voice. Oboko could only faintly see her from the distant glow reflected from the hidden fire. He kept staring out into the blackness but he wanted to comfort her for the things Arishi had said.

'Matari ...' he began, his voice low and serious.

'My husband is a blind, jealous, violent, cruel ...' she spat out each word and abruptly ceased.

In the blackness Oboko stretched forth a hand to touch the ambiguous darkness of Matari in front of him and felt a shock at feeling the soft silk of her hair. He rested his hand on her shoulder and against her neck, fingering the invisible black strands.

'Matari ...' he said again. As he leaned forward on his knees to take her in his arms he was arrested by the sudden realization that if Matari received him to comfort her she would, in fact, be verifying her husband's words. He felt frozen in the act of reaching towards some rare fruit to save it from rotting, because his very touch might cause the rot—or confirm a spoilage already there. Oboko only knew that his body had become locked, his hand still resting, now inert, on her shoulder and neck.

'There they are,' he realized she had said. Numbed, dimly aware of an immense injustice, he squatted back, withdrew his hand and looked back into the blackness. For a while he saw nothing and then, to the left of where he'd been looking, he saw a tiny point of light in the darkness. It might be anywhere from five miles to five yards away as far as Oboko could tell. But as he watched, holding himself very steady, he could see that the light was ever so slowly moving, from right to left, but presumably mostly towards them.

'It appeared fifteen minutes ago?' he asked.

'Yes.'

Forgetting for the moment the tangle of his needs, he watched the light attentively. After a minute, although he could not tell how far away it was, he felt he could estimate *when* it would arrive.

'Matari,' he said, thinking now of the other things.

'Go back now,' she said to him.

'What can I do?'

'I have been trying to decide,' she replied in a low, tight voice. 'But I must decide alone. Go.'

Reluctantly he rose to his feet. He looked once more out at the tiny point of light which, so harmless-looking, so much like a distant, irrelevant star, crept through the blackness towards them. Finally, he turned away and trudged back downwards through the snow to the others.

He seated himself again near the fire, next to Izzi, who was still slumped forward looking into the smouldering cinders.

'About forty minutes away,' Oboko said after a pause.

Izzi didn't stir.

'You never know how close he is,' he said.

'At least a full hour,' said Lord Arishi, leaning back against his rock and smiling. Oboko looked across at him. They'll have to keep refuelling the torch,' Lord Arishi went on. 'They'll go slowly to make sure there is no overlooked path off the main trail.'

'He doesn't need a torch,' said Izzi, sipping again at the cup of wine in front of him. 'He's followed me almost forty years without even opening his eyes.'

Oboko reached behind Izzi to take from their small pile of split boards a piece of kindling to poke at the fire and begin to rebuild it. He was cold.

'Of course, with only one torch,' said Lord Arishi, 'there will be at most two or three samurai. They will not challenge you tonight.'

'Now that I'm almost dead,' Izzi went on, 'my heart suddenly feels fine, my stomach is healed; even my creeping leprosy is gone.'

'They will locate our camp,' said Lord Arishi, 'so that tonight or tomorrow there will be no chance of your riding on south without having a few swords breathing in your ears, and a dozen more rapidly approaching.'

'All my life I figured he'd plant himself in my belly or bloodstream,' said Izzi, staring into the fire, 'and what's he do? Sneak up dressed in white silk.'

'Then, tomorrow during the day, there will be a surplus of time to impale you all by dusk.'

Oboko, who had been adding sticks of kindling and blowing upon the fire, looked up into Lord Arishi's cold face.

'The idea pleases you,' he said quietly.

'No more than the rest of the hunt,' Lord Arishi replied.

Izzi shook his head as if to clear it, spat into the fire and turned abruptly to Oboko.

'We should prepare now to kill them when they pass on the trail below us,' he said sharply.

Lord Arishi laughed.

'A noble idea,' he said. 'I doubt you would live to tell about it.'

'Why not?' Izzi said. 'They've got as much right to die as me.'

'Ignoti knows you can see his torch ...' Lord Arishi began, and then started laughing again.

'What's funny?'

'Will you vow not to tell anyone?' Lord Arishi asked. As Oboko's fresh kindling began to crackle and flame, Arishi's face flickered brightly; he seemed to be playing with them.

'What?' asked Izzi irritably.

'One of Ignoti's tactics when hunting at night—no one he's followed has lived to tell about it so it is a well-kept secret—is to send thirty yards ahead of the horseman with the torch a master swordsman on foot, trained, we may be sure, to move more silently than a snowflake melting down a sword blade. The hunted, of course, look for samurai trailing *behind* the "bait" with the light, but have swords sticking out of their bellies before they have the final pleasure of meeting Ignoti's master swordsman.'

'But now you have told us,' said Izzi, frowning.

'So?'

'We will ... ambush them.'

Lord Arishi sighed exaggeratedly.

'Ah, you poets,' he said. 'In your tales, two heroes—especially poets whose ability with the sword is so obviously superior to trained warriors—can always ambush three villains. Only three. But, my glorious court poet, these three *expect* an ambush, their every sense is tuned to hearing you, smelling you, feeling you, with senses I could not pretend to label. If you get within five yards of that trail—even if you kill yourself first and lie as a corpse—they will sense you, find you, and—to complete my metaphor—bury you.'

'Then what happened to your great samurai back at the temple?' Izzi asked, leaning towards Lord Arishi with a triumphant and aggressive smile.

The playful light left Lord Arishi's eyes and his face fell for a single second into a look of despair, then froze into cold concentration.

'That ... that was the greatest error I have ever made.' He paused. 'The second greatest.'

'What was?'

'When I set out after Matari it was with the simple purpose of killing her and burying her,' said Lord Arishi, not looking at either Izzi or Oboko, but beyond them both into the night. 'I brought with me then, not my two best warriors—that would have been humiliating for me—but rather an old family priest and a young samurai I have been personally training in the arts of a warrior.'

'The old man was not a warrior?' said Oboko.

'No,' said Lord Arishi, glancing just for a single moment at Oboko, then looking back beyond. 'He was wise; he had been trained briefly as a youth with the bow, but his way was the way of knowledge, not that of the warrior.'

Oboko and Izzi were both silent, Oboko leaning on his elbow before the fire, watching Lord Arishi intently. He was always aware with part of his consciousness of Matari on the high ground off in the darkness, and beyond her the approaching ... hole in the darkness. After hesitating, Lord Arishi went on:

'And although we all sensed there was something false about the situation, Izzi here seemed genuinely drunk and you, Oboko, seemed ... a harmless monk.'

'I *was* genuinely drunk,' said Izzi sharply. 'You wouldn't have found me rushing around on a big horse in the middle of a lot of swords if I'd been sober.'

'Still,' said Lord Arishi, 'the two of you out-fought us, and all day while riding I've been trying to discover how it could possibly have happened.'

'And ...?' asked Oboko in the elongated pause.

'I think I believe in luck,' replied Lord Arishi, smiling out at the darkness.

Izzi laughed.

'My personal deity,' he said, and raised his cup in toast.

'No,' frowned Arishi. 'No, luck. Our little battle was decided, as battles often are, with the first blow, the one with which Oboko wounded and disarmed Sudi.'

Oboko considered this for a moment and then said:

'He turned to look at Izzi rushing at you.' He paused to remember and analyse. 'He was concerned with you and himself, while I,' Oboko smiled, 'was only concerned with me.'

'Yes,' said Lord Arishi, frowning more deeply out at the blackness which surrounded them. 'I believe you're right. Although I have ... had been trying to train him always to be aware of the whole, never of desperate entities, I know ... he hadn't yet learned to detach himself from himself ... or me ... or ...'

'And that killed him,' said Oboko.

Lord Arishi seemed to flinch at Oboko's words.

'Our swords helped,' said Izzi and spat into the fire.

But Lord Arishi, unnoticing, slowly, as if to himself, or to the darkness out beyond, went on:

'I had brought him along with me on this ... judgement,' he said, 'because I wanted him to see ...' A second time Lord Arishi seemed to flinch, but continued. '... to see me ... decapitate my wife.'

Neither Oboko nor Izzi spoke; they watched him, his face again frozen, struggle to go on.

'He ... like many men of my court,' he said, some intense inner battle raging, but each word as it fell into the night air as cold and hard as a stone, 'he ... loved ... Matari, with a ... proper ... love, the love due to the ... beautiful wife of a great lord.'

Only the occasional soft stirring of the small fir trees

and the continual hiss of the fire punctuated the silences between Arishi's words.

'I wanted him to see the man he ... most loved,' —mouth closed, he seemed to wait patiently for the forces of speech to defeat those of silence—'kill ... decapitate ... the lady he most ... loved. That, I believed, would teach him,' Lord Arishi's face broke out into a brief hideous grin, '... would teach him ... *detachment*.'

They stared at him.

'He *cared*, you see,' Lord Arishi went on a little less painfully now, 'too much. And a samurai must, above all, care for no single creature, including himself, more than any other. Seeing me kill ... decapitate my wife would have ... helped him.'

Lord Arishi now lowered his gaze at last from the blackness beyond, and turned slightly to meet Oboko's pained gaze.

'And so, concerned with me,' he went on, 'and not seeing the whole, Sudi failed to parry your first blow, and with him disarmed, and with the old priest by chance outside, I had a more difficult time with you than I anticipated.'

'It was chance that defeated you,' said Izzi soberly.

'No,' said Arishi. 'Even one against two I should have prevailed, and about this failure also I have thought.'

He paused.

'Yes?' asked Oboko.

Staring now into the fire, Lord Arishi said nothing for several more moments.

'I, too, *cared*,' he said softly at last.

As if an hallucination had formed itself out of nothing on the blanket next to the fire between the two poets and Lord Arishi, suddenly appeared, seated, black strands of hair spilling down her white dress, Matari.

The two poets turned to look at her as at some religious statue about which they had just heard a lecture.

'The torch moved away from us and out of sight for

about five minutes,' she said, directing her words to Oboko, who had sat up, 'but now, again, it approaches.'

'Should we smother our fire,' asked Oboko to Izzi.

'What wind there is carries our smoke well off to their left,' Izzi answered. 'And this fire isn't giving enough light to be seen twenty yards away; I tested when I returned.'

'Matari ...' said Lord Arishi, still staring into the fire, but with a strange gentle expression on his face which Oboko had never seen before.

'Should I prepare the horses?' Matari asked.

'Matari ...' Lord Arishi repeated softly, his face almost beautific in the glow of the fire.

'The horses can wait,' said Izzi, beginning to get to his feet. 'They may yet stop to camp for the night.'

'Matari ...' said Lord Arishi a third time, but now looking up and staring at her. Oboko was pained by the look of love on Lord Arishi's face and was about to stammer out something, anything, when that face suddenly twisted strangely into what became after a few moments of painful silence, an absurd, tortured grin.

'Give me your head,' Arishi then said to her, who, cool, continued to look at Oboko.

'I guess it's my watch,' said Izzi, who had risen and was stretching his arms. He clomped through the snow away into the darkness.

'I want your head,' Arishi said again, grinning. Matari, holding herself erect and steady, still looked at Oboko, only her long dark lashes quivering slightly.

'Only your head Matari,' Arishi went on, leaning towards her, now aggressively. 'I won't ask for more.'

'Be quiet,' Oboko said sharply. Matari had turned her eyes to the bare earth at her feet near the fire.

'Speak to me, Matari,' Arishi said, ignoring Oboko. 'Let me see you use your mouth on me.'

Oboko stood up.

'Stop it!' he said.

'You *do* permit overnight conjugal visits to the prisoner, don't you?' Arishi said to Oboko, grinning.

'Get away from here,' Oboko said sharply. 'Go. Leave us.'

Lord Arishi rocked back and exploded into laughter. 'Leave you! Get away from here!' he echoed, laughing. 'I can't! You see, I've given an unbreakable vow.'

'Then act ... act like Lord Arishi,' said Oboko, angry. He was glaring at Arishi's mocking face over the bowed head of Matari. Then Lord Arishi's face fell into a scowl.

'Yes, well,' he said, looking away from Oboko and Matari and twisting his head from side to side nervously. His grin was gone. For a moment he sat there scowling and shaking his head and then, with surprising steadiness considering all he had drunk, he rose to his feet.

He nodded once, formally, to Oboko, glanced down once at the bowed head of Matari—and seemed to flinch. Steadying himself, he announced that he would sleep next to the horses and strode away slowly into the darkness.

Oboko, still standing, watched him disappear. Looking down at Matari, he felt his anger slowly subsiding.

'He won't try to escape?' he found himself asking.

'No,' Matari answered, in such a low voice that Oboko barely heard. Awkwardly he seated himself again cross-legged a few feet from her. As he did so Matari turned to him a look of cold hatred.

'You keep forgetting,' she said. 'We are *his* prisoners.'

Oboko had to look away at his feet, the fire, the darkness. He found he couldn't focus his mind; his every sense was attuned to the energies burning in the person five feet to his left.

'This ... trip we are taking,' he heard her saying. 'I find it impossible.'

'I ... the riding's hard, I know,' Oboko began, still not looking at her.

'Shit the riding,' Matari replied sharply, the obscenity falling from her lips seeming to Oboko as strange as if a toad had just hopped out of her mouth. 'I can ride, ride you or Izzi into your grave. I mean ... Lord Arishi ... with us.'

'Yes, I know,' said Oboko, at last meeting her eyes. Her face was softer than he'd expected.

'We can't kill him,' she said. 'I understand that. But we can leave him behind for his men.'

'I've thought of it.'

'We must.'

'But ... but what is the purpose of our journey?'

Matari looked at him blankly for a moment, her eyes widened and she showed again her anger.

'To live. That I may live.'

'Yes. And with Lord Arishi leading his men we would have no chance of reaching Lissa.'

'How can one man make that great a difference?'

Oboko only smiled.

'You know that better than I.'

Matari frowned in concentration, her eyes still meeting Oboko's steadily.

'All right, yes. You're right,' she said. She reached now for the wine-skin of saki, took it, and drank.

'Then we must do the other thing,' she went on.

'What's that?' Oboko asked.

'I am leaving, alone, tonight,' she said. Oboko started to speak but she went on. 'You and Izzi remain here with Lord Arishi and at daylight escape as best you can heading for Lissa. I shall ride south to the valley and then east away from Lissa. When Lord Arishi's men overtake you—as, of course, they will—delay as long as you can and offer to spare Lord Arishi only if you too are guaranteed safety.' She paused, then smiled coldly. 'They will accept. Lord Arishi and his men can then continue, without distraction, their great hunt.'

'You could no more escape than we.'

'But I'll have as good a chance this way as with us all remaining together in our collective madness.' Her stern look finally softened. 'And this way, you and Izzi ... may live.'

'It's impossible to move on a night like this without light.'

'Anything is possible. I've heard my husband tell of men who can walk through a totally blackened room and not strike a single vase among those scattered at random on the floor.'

'He speaks of trained samurai.'

Matari laughed.

'I am a trained woman,' she said, 'and have senses you or Arishi not only can't name but don't even know exist.'

Oboko smiled but slowly shook his head.

'It makes no difference,' she went on softly. Looking at her, he saw that the woman who had been so fierce, obscene, confident, now had tears glistening in her eyes. 'I am going, tonight, alone, no matter what you say.'

'Then ... then why do you cry?' asked Oboko gently.

'I cry because tonight, alone, I am going.'

'But—'

'And were I to stay, I would cry also. I cry because I feel like crying,' and she lowered her face into her hands and with only the smallest and most suppressed of sounds she cried.

Oboko crawled on his knees to her side and placed a hand across her back to clasp her shoulder.

'Matari ...' he said, feeling the shuddering of her small frame, hearing the strange sad sniffs and whimperings of a human being in tears. He pulled her body against his, the black silk of her hair touching the side of his face sending a knife of ecstasy stabbing through his body so that he shook.

For a minute perhaps, they were thus together, touching, trembling. Matari crying, Oboko in some ambivalent roaring state of bliss and grief, his body so charged with energy that the snow seemed to be melting around him.

Then Matari stopped crying. Her head still buried in her two moist hands, her body ceased to shudder, the sniffs and whimperings ceased. But she did not move. And Oboko, in joyful empathetic grief when she was weeping, as soon as he realized her stillness and silence, her hair yet against his face, her body tight against his, was filled with the most painful, ecstatic, terrifying anguish, for now, for now, for now . . .

'Do not mistake me,' he heard her voice say softly. 'Tonight, alone, I'm going. Being human, I weep at what I know must come, but, being Matari, I nevertheless *know* that tonight, alone, I go.'

'No,' Oboko said, and with his words he felt such a rush of certainty and bliss that he momentarily thought that someone must have come with torches, so bright seemed the world in the darkness. 'I'll never let you leave alone.'

She turned her face at last up to his. When she saw Oboko's radiant face, she stopped, turned her head slowly once to the left and once to the right as if in pain or in some slow motion negative. Tears sprang again wetly into her eyes. And for a long moment they looked at each other, Oboko seeing nothing but his love and his beloved, and Matari, older, seeing all, seeing all, and in tears.

'I love you,' Oboko whispered to her exultantly.

'No, Oboko,' she said with difficulty, again shaking her head as if a fish trying in slow motion to dislodge a hook. 'No . . . I . . .'

'They're almost here,' interrupted Izzi's harsh whisper.

In confusion Oboko stared off in the direction from which Izzi's voice had come.

'Who?' he asked stupidly.

'Arishi's men,' Izzi said back softly, appearing now nearer the fire. 'Where the hell is Arishi?' Standing at the edge of the darkness, his squat, black-bearded figure looked like some gnome.

'Arishi?' asked Oboko, looking around vaguely.

'Holy turds of Buddha!' said Izzi. 'I'm about to be attacked by killers and my army is asleep in *nirvana*.'

''Boko!' he snapped in a suppressed shout.

Matari rose swiftly and began to gather up the wine-skins, blankets and cups. Oboko, still seated, stared at her.

'I'll pack the horses,' she said and, arms full, moved off towards where they were tethered.

Izzi, standing now across the fire from Oboko, spoke to him in a subdued voice.

'Poor, stupid Oboko,' he said gently. 'When Buddha places a beautiful meal before you in the privacy of a temple, you cannot decide you are hungry. And now when the same meal is offered—no less beautiful, I admit—only with a sword blade hanging inches above the plate and already falling, you suddenly ...' Izzi shook his head.

Oboko, still dazed, looked across at him.

'I love Matari,' he said, as if testing the idea.

'Don't we all,' said Izzi, and his laughter broke once, a half snort, from a mouth that was mostly a pained grimace.

'But ... my love ... is pure,' said Oboko, as if, again, testing an idea.

Izzi's eyes were wet with tears or laughter.

'Oh *maya, Mara, maya,* spare him, spare him,' he said.

'What do you—'

'Your mouth seeks the same mouth, your spit the same spit, your prick goes in the same hole.'

Oboko stood up.

'They're coming?' he said, shaking his head sharply as if to clear it.

'Coming!?' snapped Izzi. 'They've probably already seen us, surrounded us and killed us. It's certain you'd never have noticed.'

Oboko patted his sword, kicked a little snow on to the fire to reduce its light and then moved quietly to Izzi.

'I seem ...' he began, but stopped abruptly. 'Let us go.'

They moved away from the fire, up around the large boulder and across some tightly packed snow, Izzi leading, Oboko following, his body still tingling, trembling, but his mind numb. After only a few seconds they arrived at the top of the little protective ridge and looked down through the darkness towards the trail.

A torch blazed not more than thirty yards away from them to the west. They could see the outline of a rider and a horse. Kneeling side by side in the foot deep snow, they peered over a rock at the torch and rider who seemed to be exactly where the path which Oboko and Matari had masked left the trail to lead up towards the camp.

The light had stopped moving. Between its glare and them the dark outline of a second man on horseback appeared. He was riding, slowly, up the incline directly towards them. Almost in the same motion Oboko and Izzi silently drew their swords. The horseman seemed already twenty feet off the main trail and clearly past the ten feet of trampled snow which Oboko and Matari had purposely not covered over. With the light behind him the figure of the horseman was totally black; where he was looking it was impossible to tell. He walked his horse onward yet another ten or fifteen feet towards them. Already, Oboko guessed, he might be able to see the part of their trampled path to the camp which he and Matari had not bothered to disguise. Another five feet he came. Then he stopped.

The horseman, silent, was sitting outlined against the more distant torch about halfway to them from the trail, only forty feet away. For all they could tell he was staring right at them as they peered at him over the rock; whether he could see them they couldn't tell. For fifteen seconds, twenty, thirty, the horseman sat there, black, without making the slightest movement. Then, gently, without hurry he turned his horse and slowly let it walk him back to the horseman with the torch on the main trail. A reprieve.

'Living Buddha,' whispered Izzi, 'I think I shit in my pants.'

'He saw us,' said Oboko.

'If he'd seen my face, he'd have known all he had to

do was glare at me and I'd have rolled over dead.'

'Look,' said Oboko softly.

The horseman with the torch was now slowly moving forward to the south, following the trail Izzi had created around past the pinnacle. The black horseman, last seen to the right and behind the man with the torch, could no longer be seen. He had disappeared, presumably following the first man at a distance.

The light vanished for half a minute to their left behind a rise, but re-emerged further on, still following Izzi's trail.

'How long before they'll have circled round and arrived at our camp from behind?' Oboko asked.

'Thirty, forty minutes,' Izzi replied. 'If that's what they're really doing.'

They both stared into the blackness left by the departed torch. Oboko doubted that the black horseman was waiting down there; he felt that if they were going to ambush the camp, they would all do it, not just one.

'Do you think they all went?' Izzi asked. 'Or is that black horseman just sitting there waiting for me to close my eyes?'

'I'm going to go and look,' said Oboko. He started to crawl up over the rock behind which they had been kneeling, but felt Izzi pulling back on the end of his cloak. Oboko stopped and looked back at Izzi, whose face he couldn't see at all.

'You don't have to go to *Him*,' Izzi said in a hoarse whisper, 'He comes to you.'

'We've got to know where they are,' Oboko answered urgently, 'if one of them is *there*. If they have all moved on I'll follow until they stop for the night or until they reach the other entrance to our camp.'

Izzi was silent.

'All right,' he said after several seconds. 'But if they begin to approach that other entrance, we'll have to ride out this way. If they don't kill us we'll meet you at the base of the pinnacle.'

Staring back at Izzi without speaking, Oboko considered his words. Then he turned away to continue crawling up over the rock until he was able to scramble silently to his feet. As he started stumbling through the blackness towards the trail, he could see that the retreating light—it was already too distant to be called a torch—was far off to his left. But where the black horseman was, Buddha alone might know.

Ten

Oboko moved through the night not like a cat but like a small clumsy bear, banging his legs against large rocks, falling twice into the soft snow and once against a boulder, bruising the forearm that he had thrust forward for protection. He moved silently, however, suppressing grunts of pain and happy sounds of amused frustration, and headed towards a spot on the main trail well to the right of where he'd last seen the black horseman. There he could hike back to the left after the retreating light and at the same time determine whether any of the samurai had remained behind. The thought flashed briefly through Oboko's mind that his method of determining whether the black horseman was waiting for him was simply to see if he, Oboko, survived. If he were suddenly killed, this would be strong evidence that the black horseman had not followed the other. He smiled to himself as he ploughed through the black snow he could not see. Absurdity upon absurdity. But blissful, beautiful absurdity. Feeling himself eternal, Oboko found that the thought of sudden death seemed rather amusing. All of life seemed overwhelmingly perfect, including that minor trivial inconvenience called death.

Reaching at last the trampled snow where horses had passed, he found in looking to his left that he could no longer see any light. He could see almost nothing. He stood at the edge of the area of crushed snow, immobile, his eyes, ears, nose, and skin all reaching out into the darkness around him to finger for signs of waiting death. He sensed nothing: a light warm breeze against his face from the south, a tiny whir of air sighing through pine branches somewhere near, a small sinking feeling as his right boot pressed another half-inch into the snow. His breath came smoothly and silently. He was serene. He 'felt' he was alone.

Able to make out shades of darkness a few feet in front of him—utter blackness where the snow had been disturbed, ever so slightly less where it was smooth and regular and reflective of the moon's almost totally blanketed light—he began walking rapidly to the south. His body seemed to him aflame, sometimes with absurd joy, sometimes with the acute effort to expand his senses beyond their normal capabilities to 'feel' the world in a way he'd never done before.

He had moved without incident fifty or sixty feet, still without seeing any light ahead of him, when the trail apparently bent at an angle to the right and he blundered into a tree. He knocked the breath out of himself, but as soon as he was sure he hadn't been struck down by the black horseman, he rose cheerfully to his feet and continued onwards.

After another three minutes, however, he still could not see any torch ahead of him. He slowed his pace, considering whether they had stopped and were waiting in the darkness to kill him. As he bent into a defensive crouch, a boot creaked as it dug deeper into the snow. His senses straining to pick up the scent or sound of death, Oboko waited for thirty seconds, feeling and smelling and hearing only the breeze. Finally, guessing, hoping that the absence of their light all this time was because he was still too far behind them, he again hurried on, still walking rather than trotting, his sword now held in his cold right hand.

He walked on and on, twice stumbling into deep snow, once grunting aloud when his rib cage struck a rock. After another ten minutes he still hadn't seen the torch and was certain that the trail must be beginning to circle back northwards and their horses might begin to smell him behind them. His serene joyfulness had moderated somewhat, as had his expanding senses. He experienced brief periods of great fatigue. Still, he went on. He was thinking of what delicate and intelligent noses horses must have when—it seemed so absurd as to be an event from nightmare or dream—he bumped into a horse's rear end.

The rear end was moving, but Oboko's face brushed the tail and his knee struck a hind leg. Oboko stopped dead, the horse leaped forward two strides and gave a short loud nervous whinny. Standing still, Oboko could hear the horse stamp through the snow and, now, hear it stop moving. Everything was silent. Even the wind seemed to be resting.

He guessed that the horse hadn't been turned around and imagined that the rider was poised, sword in hand, listening as carefully as Oboko to the enemy he must know had disturbed his horse and must be standing, as indeed Oboko was, twelve feet away in the darkness. Oboko considered running, but didn't like the thought of turning his back to the invisible horseman.

'Chk-chk,' a voice said about thirty feet in front of him, and Oboko heard the sound of a horse moving—closer than the voice it seemed—but moving away. Well.

He remained where he was, listening to the sounds of movement through the snow until they were lost in the distance—fifty feet away?

So.

Oboko was certain that *they, he,* the invisible black horseman, knew he was behind them. Thus he, they, must be waiting, calmly, a dozen yards up the trail to . . .

Oboko was sweating. He found it difficult to remember what he was doing here. He felt dizzy. He couldn't go on. There seemed no sense in going on. His feet felt very comfortable in the exact snow where he happened to be standing. Unless . . . unless the horse's sudden movement and whinny had been interpreted as a stumble; the black stallion had stumbled and snorted a dozen times during the day. Why else had the rider revealed his presence by calling softly to his horse? Oboko felt uncertainty. Fear. Somehow he found himself moving silently forward, not particularly fast, but forward, stopping every ten steps to listen and smell and feel into the darkness, his senses not aflame as they had been earlier, but tense, torn, tingling with fear.

He advanced fifteen feet. Twenty-five feet. Forty feet. Fifty feet. He was still alive. He began to move slightly faster. Sixty feet. Eighty. Then, before him, outlined clearly for a single instant against the at last appearing distant torch, a horse and rider, leading, he could just for that instant see, a second, riderless horse. He stopped and watched.

The torch was stationary, lighting a single horseman and horse, and the other two horses moved on towards it. Oboko continued forward now more rapidly for ten long strides when he halted abruptly in terror. Why had they stopped so obviously? Had they only now lit the torch? Why? *Where was the third samurai?* Now trembling violently, he suddenly sensed a few feet to his right some strange darkness in the dark. Had it moved even? He felt he knew what it must be and, raising his sword, he crouched and turned his upper body to face it. The darkness didn't move nor make a sound. The sweat covering Oboko's cold face increased his shivering and he strained his eyes to see: only a darkness in the dark. He tried to attune his other senses to that spot but fear blurred and distorted everything. Without further thinking, he finally leaped forward and plunged his sword into that darkness.

He felt his sword strike rock and ricochet upwards and to the left as he himself stumbled and hit the rock hard with his hip. He lived. The darkness within the darkness had not been there, and he lived.

No longer trembling, he quickly rose to look again up the trail. The torch was where it had been and now both of the two samurai he'd seen had dismounted; one seemed to be grouping the three horses near a tree. The samurai with the torch then moved away on foot to the right and there, by the light of the torch, Oboko saw—now all was clear to him—both the third samurai and the huge pinnacle-shaped rock which marked the furthest point that Izzi was to have ridden in his circle back to the camp. Here, cutting off their escape route south to Lissa, the three warriors, as wise as Lord Arishi had warned them they would be, had chosen to camp for the night. They were ignoring the fact that Izzi's trail led onwards to the east, ignoring their probable knowledge of precisely where their prey's camp was, ignoring their awareness of Oboko's blundering along in the darkness following them, and simply camping in the one single spot where they shouldn't camp. In the morning, there would be twenty or so horsemen on one side of Oboko and the others, and these three well trained and fully prepared warriors waiting to stop their escape to the south. Oboko, Matari, and Izzi could eat their breakfast at dawn—always the privilege of those about to be executed—and then die.

Oboko walked almost calmly another forty feet closer, until he was only a dozen yards away from the tethered horses. There he stood silently and listened to the three men exchange a few words which confirmed his interpretation of their camping where they were for the night. Finally, numb, he wheeled and headed back through the night towards Matari.

He strode along with his eyes fixed on the dimly visible blackness of trampled snow, his mind numb, exhaustion flooding through his body like a lake released at last from its confinement by a fallen dam. He might for a second time have walked at full stride into a horse except that this time his left arm only brushed the foot of the rider. A horse again whinnied.

Oboko leaped away and fell into the snow, jamming his hand which was reaching for his sword, but rolling over once and springing to his feet.

'I am Lady Arishi,' came Matari's firm voice, and Oboko, sword in hand, seeing before him only the darkness, realized that she thought he was one of her husband's samurai.

'Matari,' he whispered. 'What ...?'

'Oboko?'

Stretching a bare hand in front of him, Oboko moved forward until he felt the rump of the horse. The horse shuddered but did not move. Oboko slid along the side of the horse until he touched at last her boot in the stirrup.

'Yes, Matari, Oboko,' he said.

'Where are ... they?' she asked in a low voice.

'Camped at the pinnacle,' he said, holding one hand gently on the smooth cold leather of her boot, the other sheathing his sword.

Matari was silent. As he waited for her to speak he abruptly realized why she was here: she had, as she said she would, left them to flee south alone.

'The others?' he asked her for confirmation.

'They ... they are in camp,' she replied.

'There's no way past them,' Oboko said softly, staring upwards into the darkness where she must be sitting. But seeing nothing. He felt serene again, untired. The touch of her boot to his hand was a caress.

Matari was again silent. The horse—Oboko felt from its size it was the big stallion—shook its head slightly, the reins making tiny slapping sounds against his neck.

'We must go back together,' Oboko went on.

But Matari remained wordless. He sensed her sitting there erect above him staring south past the invisible samurai and pinnacle to the distant horizon, towards which he could feel her straining.

Her low voice finally broke the silence, as if addressing herself.

'When ... will I be free?' she said.

Oboko stared blindly up at her, but she didn't go on.

'We can only sleep,' he said. 'Tomorrow, at dawn, then ...' but he wasn't up to finishing the sentence.

Matari didn't reply, but in a few moments she must have tugged gently on the reins, for the horse began to turn to his right, Oboko moving slowly around with it. He reached upwards to grasp the reins and without words, Matari let him take them and lead the horse and her back to the camp and Lord Arishi.

Eleven

And so, exhausted, with nothing to be feared or done until dawn, they tried to sleep. Lord Arishi slept alone, as he had started to do earlier, by the horses. Oboko, Izzi, and Matari made little cradles in the snow around the fire to fit their bodies and, each wrapped in a blanket, curled up like foetuses to sleep. First the two men had discussed whether they should try to kill the three samurai, but quickly concluded that, besides being reluctant to kill unnecessarily, and besides the probability of themselves being victims rather than murderers, they were both too tired to do another thing. They even agreed not to take turns sleeping on the high ground on watch since it was so dark that one of the three samurai would be whispering love words into an ear before he'd be noticed. Instead both curled up by the fire. Exhaustion had made them fatalists: they would live to see the next dawn or not; so tired were they that the outcome seemed less important than being able to sleep.

For his usual fifteen minutes Oboko tried to perform his evening meditation, but it was impossible. At first he kept losing count of his breaths because he was too acutely aware of Matari curled up a few feet away, facing him, perhaps not yet asleep. Then he lost his sense of breathing because, although still sitting there erect and fierce-looking, he kept falling asleep. Finally all proper awareness of his meditation was destroyed by the overwhelming conviction that meditation was a waste of time, a thought that had not entered his mind for two years. He turned numbly to his nightly poem.

He was again at first distractingly aware of Matari lying in the snow beside him, of Izzi slumbering noisily a few yards in front. Next he found that his mind had become as totally blank as it was supposed to have been when he was trying to meditate. Only after many minutes did he suddenly have a vision of Matari, and he leaned forward and inked out his words:

Wet eyes in the firelight
The touch of a strand of hair.
How full I am.

He folded up the paper, stuffed it, his pen, and ink into his small bag, and curled up into sleep.

*

Later, much later—it was after he had slept for many hours but long before dawn—Oboko found himself awake, staring up into the darkness, complete now, for there were not even a few glowing coals left of the fire, and he heard—or had it been a dream, no, he heard—the voice of Matari. It came from his left, and hearing it made him feel that they had been lying side by side awake for hours.

'When I was a young girl,' she was saying softly, 'I was afraid of nights as black as this ...' She paused, and Oboko, lying half on his side, lifted his face slightly to look in her direction. He could see nothing. 'But now,' she went on, 'when death lies on every side of me, I *like* the blackness. It seems like warm walls are all about.'

'Not so warm,' said Oboko.

'Warm in other ways,' she replied. 'Warm, I suppose, from you and Izzi being on either side of me.'

Oboko felt himself saying (but didn't say aloud) that

Izzi and he were not much of a protection from the other blacknesses further away. He said nothing.

'It's strange you should be so brave,' Matari then said meditatively.

'I'm not brave,' Oboko replied quickly.

'I'm not flattering,' she said, her voice low but not a whisper. 'I simply find it strange. For so much of you is a monk, so much of you a poet, I'm surprised there's any place left for a warrior.'

Oboko became aware of all the space he had suddenly found available for the lover and, with awareness, he felt the space fill. He could feel his face becoming flushed. The thought of her lying in the darkness only a few feet from him, her soft voice seeming to breathe against his ear, set him shivering. He clenched his fists and stomach muscles to try to control it and began to concentrate on his breathing. His efforts were interrupted by the sound of her soft laughter.

'The only thing I can see you fear is me,' she said.

He felt a thrust of resentment at her accuracy, or perhaps at her laughter. His abdomen was rising nicely with the inhale and he concentrated on holding his breath in for many seconds.

'Ah, 'Boko, I'm sorry,' Matari went on. 'The flirt in me will not die, even with the blade kissing my neck.'

Oboko was silent. He hadn't noticed that she was flirting. Was she?

'But of course it isn't flirtation,' she said.

They were both silent now and, with the fire extinguished and the night now windless, the only sound was a steady rhythmic buzz: Izzi was quietly snoring beyond their feet. Oboko didn't find the silence uncomfortable; it was warm. Matari's voice was soft and reassuring and unmocking: he sensed no flirting in anything she said. He imagined that awake, she, like him, felt a need to have human contact: the touch, at least, of voices in the dark.

'How strange is snow,' he heard her say softly.

'Yes,' he said, becoming aware as he spoke that his left

hand, snuggled under his beard, was pressed not against a blanket but against packed snow.

'All my life,' she went on in a dreamlike voice, 'snow has been white flakes drifting harmlessly across the sky, always lovely to look at, lovely to touch. But three nights ago snow was white earth the sky seemed to be shovelling down to bury me.'

'And I a grave-digger,' said Oboko.

'Yes,' she said. Izzi's rhythmic buzzing was abruptly interrupted by two brief coughs, then, as Oboko and Matari listened, it resumed.

'And now, tonight,' Matari went on, 'snow is a bed softer and warmer in many ways than any I have known for years.'

Oboko pushed his blanket away from his neck and adjusted his position so that he was lying on his back, eyes open facing the black centre of the heavens.

'The snow,' he said slowly, 'is also the white curtain God may draw down from the sky to hide the next act of the play.' It was that, he thought, examining his own line. The thick layer of clouds which blanketed the moon and stars must hold something for them next day.

'The snow is also,' he heard Matari saying, 'the white sheet of paper across which as we move we scrawl our unending and all-revealing signatures.'

Oboko, whose eyes had been closed, now opened them again to stare unseeing up at the blackness above.

'Snow is the spring blossom of the evergreen,' he said automatically.

'Snow is the silk shroud in which I may be buried,' said Matari.

Neither of them said anything for several moments, Oboko hearing for the first time since awakening the soft sound of the wind stirring in the pines.

'Why "silk"?' Oboko found himself asking.

He heard Matari laugh softly.

'You wouldn't expect Lady Arishi to be buried in mere "cotton" snow, would you?' and again she laughed.

They again both lapsed into silence, Oboko becoming aware that Izzi's snoring was almost like the sound of surf sliding in rhythmic rolls upon the sand.

'When I was a girl,' Matari began again slowly but in a voice so low he could barely hear it, 'I used to daydream all the time of dying some tragic death and being carried dressed in my most beautiful white silk gown through the crowded city streets of Kyoto. Thousands there would mourn my death and stand in awe of my beauty. My lover ...' she hesitated, and for a moment Oboko thought her voice had become so low he could no longer hear her. '... my lover, who tended in my daydreams to change from month to month over the years, would be overwhelmed at his guilt—although it wasn't too clear why he was responsible for my death. As I passed on my bier he would fall upon his sword in anguish.'

'How did you die?' asked Oboko.

Matari didn't reply right away.

'I don't remember,' she said after a pause. 'Actually I do. I died of being wronged—a disease very popular in the tales told by our poets when I was young.' She was speaking now in a firmer, clearer voice.

'Of being wronged ...' mused Oboko. He opened his eyes to let his vision fall into the blackness above.

'Yes,' she said quietly. 'I would be falsely accused of something and then, just as everyone was discovering my innocence, I would conveniently die.'

'But in real life,' said Oboko slowly, after a brief silence, 'you prefer to live.'

'Real life,' replied Matari in her low voice, 'has, I have found, no connection whatsoever with the world of poets.'

Oboko laughed.

'Perhaps you have only read bad poets.'

'Perhaps,' she said. Then added, after a stretch of silence broken only by the sound of Izzi's breaths breaking upon the black beach of the night, 'Perhaps the good ones are too painful to read.'

And then, apparently, they had both slept. At least

Oboko remembered no more when he awoke. But his awakening was confused, because he was deep in some dream about a great, wandering sage—himself partly, partly Master Eno? and partly, how strange! Izzi—who was moving down an endless mountain, but as he walked, his each step made a strange, frightening scraping sound: 'shhhlk! shhhlk! shhhlk!' at each stride down the mountain. And yet, even though the great wandering sage—it wasn't Master Eno, no, not him—was always striding downwards, he never seemed to get closer to, closer to ... to, what was it?

Oboko awoke in daylight to see Izzi seated in front of him, a blanket draped over the top of his head, staring in total fascination at something on the other side of Oboko.

'Now, at last, I know what he looks like,' Izzi said, as Oboko rubbed his eyes and still seemed to hear the 'shhhlk! shhhlk!' of his dream.

'Who?' Oboko asked, struggling to free his arm from the blanket and sit up.

'Him,' said Izzi, still staring past Oboko in expressionless concentration. Oboko managed to sit up. 'The little dwarf on my back,' added Izzi, and Oboko now turned to his left to see, past Matari who was also sitting up and looking where Izzi stared, the figure of Lord Arishi, neutral, inevitable, seated with his back against a rock, across his knees his huge great sword, across which he rubbed, back and forth, a sharpening stone: 'shhhlk! shhhlk!'

'Death,' added Izzi, but neither Oboko nor Matari, watching in silence, needed any explanation of what they saw.

Twelve

It was already an hour after the first hint of grey had rimmed the eastern horizon when the four of them shared the last of the rice and wine, fed the horses, and prepared to go on. The sun hadn't risen that day. Rather a gradual grey had emerged out of the blackness in the east, spread like an opaque dome across the sky until, when they awoke, they were enclosed in it: a grey heavy covering which, during the course of the long day would grow no lighter in colour and no less oppressive, until in the late afternoon it began to spill at last its great weight on to the world below.

Oboko, Izzi and Matari had, together, decided their course of action. They expected that all three of Arishi's horsemen were remaining at or near the pinnacle. Izzi was to ride alone again along the main trail until he was seen by one or more of the samurai, who, when they saw Izzi appear and retreat, would go after him. They would not all desert the narrow pass south which they blocked, but one certainly would, and probably two. Izzi would then circle back, being followed, and reapproach the pinnacle from the other side. Meanwhile, Oboko, Matari and Lord Arishi would already have approached the pinnacle by that way and would ... would do what they could and what they must to get past the last, hopefully single samurai.

Izzi, after breakfasting gaily on the last of the horsemeat, joked through the discussion of their plans and, when he was ready to leave, gave a mock salute to the stony-faced Lord Arishi.

'Goodbye, great lord,' he said boisterously. 'I'll try not to kill any of your men.'

'You will succeed,' Lord Arishi answered dryly.

'Are you ready?' Oboko asked Izzi, nervous about his strange saki-less gaiety.

'Ready, friend,' said Izzi, pulling on the reins of his horse to make it rear suddenly, 'to canter away into the dawn as bait for the jackels.'

'You are not afraid?' Oboko half asked, half said, smiling.

'No,' replied Izzi, his eyes bright and playful. 'I leave the dwarf behind with you. Of course, unfortunately,' and he turned his horse and set it walking away, 'I shall return.' He turned his head once. 'Farewell, Matari. Do not breathe too violently on the poet of the wind.'

Oboko watched him ride slowly down the rock-strewn, snow-covered slope and, once on the trail, begin to trot south-west towards an eventual meeting with the samurai somewhere at or before the pinnacle. Looking directly south, Oboko could just see it, jutting there grey and lifeless in the bleak light of early morning. Turning to look back across the open plane to the north, he could see no sign of more horsemen. He and Matari mounted the black horse, Arishi the white, and they moved slowly away to the south-west where they too, sooner or later, would have a meeting.

It felt strange to Oboko to be seeing again. When a windswept rock or scrub pine occasionally broke the monotony of snow, it seemed brighter to him than it should under the heavy sky. His senses were also sharpened by his awareness that they might, at any moment along this trampled path which Izzi had made returning the evening before, come upon one or more of the samurai. In fact, it seemed likely that one of them might even now be either following the path towards them or already have seen them and be waiting, ahead, somewhere, to ...

He stopped his horse and asked Lord Arishi and Matari to dismount. He wanted to be holding his short sword at Lord Arishi's side should anyone suddenly appear; he wanted to discourage the shooting of arrows. Matari would ride alone on the white horse and he and Arishi, despite their combined weight, would follow on the big stallion.

Thus mounted, they went on, Matari riding fifteen, then twenty yards in the lead. They rode slowly, Oboko stiff and tense behind the huge and rigid body of Lord Arishi. At first Oboko held the reins, but after less than a minute Lord Arishi, with a muttered curse when the horse swerved at an unintended tug, took them away. After a few precarious moments, Oboko found himself riding along with his arms around Lord Arishi, like ... a woman? a prisoner? In any case, he scowled.

They rode forward in silence, without being able to see the pinnacle since they had first descended from the high ground of their camp. Oboko did not want to reach the pinnacle before Izzi, nor too much later. They simply went on, the horses at a walk, Matari, slender, graceful atop the white mare, not once looking back; Oboko and Arishi, together, the one's arms around the other, eyes always forward, following her.

Whose intention it was was unclear, but Oboko noticed that gradually Matari had moved out thirty, forty, and then fifty yards in front of them, so that at times she was lost from their line of sight. As he started to spur the stallion forward at a faster pace, he glanced towards his right and saw, for the first time since leaving camp, the pinnacle; it was less than one hundred yards away. He had Lord Arishi halt the horse so that both of them could dismount and continue forward on foot. Arishi held the reins of the horse, Oboko, sword drawn, walked beside him.

When they reached the top of a little rise they could suddenly see everything: thirty yards away stood two samurai, swords drawn, watching Matari advance towards them slowly on her horse. There was no sign of either Izzi or the third samurai. A dozen yards away from the pinnacle, tethered to a small tree, there were only two horses. Since the samurai had apparently not seen them, Oboko motioned Lord Arishi to remain hidden and immobile behind the partial covering of a small fir tree a few paces in front of them.

'Your plan fails,' Lord Arishi said in a low, neutral voice.

Oboko only watched. Matari, approaching the samurai from left to right in front of them, could be seen in partial profile, erect and expressionless. At last, ten feet from them, she stopped. The two samurai, both small men, stood side by side, staring up at her.

'Lord Arishi awaits you,' Oboko heard her voice say, unusually loud and imperious.

The two men continued to stare at her. One of them finally said:

'Where is he?'

'Bound to a tree a mile back on the high ground.'

The two samurai exchanged a glance.

'And where are the others?'

'The other two took another trail,' Matari replied, looking down at them coldly.

Now the one who had done the speaking looked uncertainly off to his left past Oboko and Arishi, and then, a second time, to his companion.

'We can't let you pass, my lady,' he said.

'I shall pass.'

'We cannot let you.'

'My movements are not your business,' Matari said, holding herself and her horse so steady she might have been posing for a portrait. 'If Lord Arishi wishes to kill me he wishes to do it himself.'

'We do not speak of killing you.'

Matari drew out Lord Arishi's short sword from her saddle. In her tiny hand it seemed immense.

'You *know* me,' she said slowly. 'If you wish to stop me you will have to kill me ... or die.'

Watching her, neither of them moved or replied.

'Go to Lord Arishi,' she said. 'You know how he loves

the hunt. Think how angry with you he would be if by some accident you, without him, should now capture me. And of course if I am killed ...' Oboko could see that she was smiling down at them ironically.

The two samurai looked at each other a third time.

'You may pass, Lady Arishi,' said the older one, 'but Uguru must go with you.'

'It doesn't matter,' she said simply. 'But please bring me some rice cakes and something to drink.'

The younger, sheathing his sword, turned and went away to the right towards the remains of a fire, presumably for food and wine. As he stooped over a sack, Matari suddenly spurred her horse forward towards the two tethered horses, slashed through their reins, slapped one on the flank with the flat of her sword and then drove her horse forward into the crevice formed by the pinnacle and another boulder, pulling the reins of the second horse along beside her.

The older samurai leaped over to his bow, notched an arrow, and gathered Matari into his sights.

'No!' boomed Lord Arishi's voice from beside Oboko.

Oboko saw the samurai turn and see Lord Arishi walking towards him, Oboko behind, sword drawn and steady in Arishi's back, leading the black stallion. Matari had disappeared beyond the pinnacle.

'Where's Ignoto?' Lord Arishi asked the older samurai when they had drawn near; the younger was again beside the other.

'Following the other horseman,' the older man said. Although he had no beard his face was haggard and unshaven. Oboko suddenly realized that these men must find all this ... inconvenient.

'We are passing through,' Oboko said. 'Move.'

The two samurai didn't move. Swords drawn, they simply continued to look at Lord Arishi. He too ignored Oboko.

'When Ignoto returns,' he said, 'tell him that I'll be

going on for a while but will join you ... at the cherry blossoms. I, alone, shall kill Matari.'

Oboko nudged Arishi tentatively with the end of the sword. Arishi didn't move.

'And tell him to bring wine,' Lord Arishi went on. 'We have a poet with us who seems all belly.'

Having apparently said all that needed saying, Lord Arishi began walking, past his two samurai and along the path which Matari had taken with the two horses. As Oboko followed close behind, a noise made him turn. He saw Izzi galloping through the shallow snow from where they'd just come, sword held high, as if charging down on helpless peasants. The two samurai at last moved, quickly, backing out of his way, and Izzi, beaming, swirled past them. He reined in triumphant beside Oboko and Lord Arishi.

'We did it!' he announced loudly, his breath exploding in violent puffs. 'I think I'll become a captain of samurai.' He sheathed his unbloodied sword.

'We'll see,' said Lord Arishi, and Oboko hurried them all onwards to meet Matari.

Thirteen

And so, onwards, to the south, under the great grey roof of cloud which lay always just above their heads, through the untouched snow which swept in endless lovely white planes before them, they rode. Although they alternated whose horse was to push through the snow first, Oboko always rode last, with a great bow held by a single knot to the side of the samurai's brown gelding. Matari, small upon the large black stallion, guided it with such grace and sureness over the uneven depths of snow and hidden rocks that it seemed as though it had travelled the path a hundred times. Arishi again rode the white mare and Izzi the grey, but despite their now having a horse for each of them, their shadows, the two samurai now following them, seemed, with no apparent effort and frequent pauses, to remain always a hundred yards behind. Whenever Oboko turned in his saddle to check their position, they always seemed to be at rest, side by side, just out of range of accuracy of Oboko's bow, watching him with the serene, detached, unhurried look of men who already see the end of the trail even though Oboko could not. One of them, he knew, was Ignoto; the other was the younger samurai.

At noon, at last, they reached, it seemed, the end of the world. The barren, high, snow-covered plateau over which they had been struggling, suddenly ceased; they found themselves staring out over layer upon layer of an entirely new universe: a long winding path down through evergreens; more distant, the great green valley —grey-green under the heavy sky—of Lissa; beyond and to the right the grey indistinct mass of the small city; and beyond all, stretching from one end of the horizon to the next, not clearly visible in the haze and gloom, but somehow, for all of them, there, the sea.

They could even note, not more than two miles distant, it seemed, the end of the snow line, the brown and green and rust of bare earth. The warm breeze which still blew from the sea into their faces became immediately a few degrees warmer when they reached the ridge. The only thing separating them now from the warmth and safety and civilization of Lissa was twenty miles of grey sky, beneath which lay perhaps twenty miles of winding rock and gorge, mud and pine, snow and stream, and the eternal shadow of the samurai.

When Oboko looked back for the two horsemen, he saw that they had ridden off to the right and now they too, a hundred yards to the side, stood staring down into the grey-green valley, which, paradoxically, was no doubt already aburst with the growths of spring. Behind them on the long sweep of snow of the plateau they had just crossed there was still no sign of more horsemen, although he could not now see, nor had he at any time during the day more than a mile back.

After feeding briefly on the last of the rice and dried fish, as off to their side the two samurai ate, they began their descent towards the sea. Now they made better progress. Although in a few places snow drifts breasted their horses and they had to dismount and lead them through, the horses plunged and staggered down the twisting, pine-enclosed trail more rapidly than they had crossed the plateau. Once, when Matari and her black stallion came ploughing down a slope into a clearing, a tiny cluster of birds scattered skywards from beside a rock: they were the first sign of animal life they had seen.

And then the trail began to run alongside the left bank of a small stream. Although snow still lay heaped in little cones on the rocks, and snow-covered ice often bridged between, even without stopping their horses they could hear underneath the low gurgle of flowing water, and, as they descended, here and there it broke free and ran, black and urgent, among the rocks, downwards, towards the sea.

They no longer stopped for brief rests as they had, but without exchanging words with one another silently urged their mounts forward. The stream beside them deepened into a small gorge; the bridges of ice became more rare. The sound of the water changed from the low murmured gurgles it had first been to a steady, unbroken, rushing hiss.

And now the pines, which had been their silent audience since they first left the plateau, lost the clumps of snow which had nested heavily in their branches, and loomed up an unbroken green towards the grey sky. Shrubs, leafless, appeared, and here and there shrubs emitting the first tiny sparks of green buds.

The snow was now much less deep and was melting. The hooves of the horses kicked up mud, which lay, after they had passed, in ugly brown splotches on the white. But even as they joyed in the increasing ease with which their horses trotted, whenever they turned to look back, there rode the two horsemen.

After a while the gorge beside them became deep, a narrow steep crevice falling from beside their trail to the now almost totally black rushing water. Wherever there was space for the sun to reach, the path they were following was bare; only back among the pines and shrubs was the ground still buried in white. They had passed the snow line.

At last they had to halt: Izzi's grey horse had begun to lag well behind the others in exhaustion. They dismounted and fed the horses the last of what they had to give them and let them lap at the water which lay in pools in the mud by their hooves. No one spoke. While Lord Arishi looked back at the two samurai sitting immobile on a rise a hundred yards back and Izzi tended his grey mare, Oboko and Matari went and stood staring into the gorge.

The earth dropped away abruptly almost seventy feet to the rock stream where the water rushed southwards to the sea. Behind them to their right and below them to their left stretched the gorge, straight for fifty yards then bending right or left, then angling again and again and again. They knew that the only crossing was at the bottom of the valley, where, half a mile from the sea, a bridge connected Lissa to the villages to the east. On the other side of the gorge quarter of a mile distant, as well as behind them across their trail on their own side, loomed cliff-faces which seemed from where they stood to be impassable; everything seemed to be funnelling their descent directly down to the sea.

Looking in that direction from their resting place, they saw that the valley now, at last, even under the sodden sky, appeared green and bright and alive. It stretched before them like a welcoming carpet, softening the broad plane to the sea, which, unmistakable now, a deep grey, disappearing outwards into the distant sky.

They were about to return to their horses when suddenly Matari fell to her knees. There, tiny against a massive boulder, was a single purple wild flower. She reached forth a hand to pick it, hesitated, and looked up at Oboko uncertainly. The wild flower would die, of course, within a day or two in any case, but ... Matari, her long black hair falling free and wild about her face from the long day's riding, stared without expression up into Oboko's eyes for several seconds, almost as if she weren't looking at him but at something else. She looked back at the flower and this time Oboko saw her slowly smile, reach out a trembling hand until it was only a few inches away. Abruptly she stood, let the flower live, and wheeled briskly back to mount her horse.

Oboko, weighing much less, shifted to Izzi's horse, and they rode on, Matari now always in the lead, the big stallion ploughing through the muddy earth in huge, confident strides. They were now moving too rapidly to have any further worry about an arrow finding one of them from the samurai so they rarely paused to look back. The shrubs were now all abud, pink, green, and yellow against the black velvet winter branches. Their descent, now less uneven, more gradual, more certain, took them spattering through the mud, bursting through low budding shrubs, over tiny, invisible wild flowers, across rotting logs, past the decaying carcass of some animal killed during the winter only to be reborn with the melting of the snow as a corpse.

After another half-hour they stopped again to rest, this time in front of a giant pine tree which, apparently struck by lightning—its roots, trunk, and green needles all seemed to be flourishing still—had fallen not only across their trail but also all the way across the gorge, its topmost branches wedged between two rocks on the far side. There was no difficulty at all in going to the left around the fallen tree, but Matari, in the lead, stopped and, smiling fully for the first time that day, turned to await the others.

Izzi arrived, the brown gelding he now rode snorting and rearing, and then Lord Arishi, stern and unspeaking, and at last Oboko, his exhausted grey barely maintaining a trot.

'Are we blocked?' Oboko asked.

'No, no, no,' answered Matari, still smiling. 'Look!'

She was staring off behind them from where they'd come and they all turned to follow her gaze. It took several seconds to locate the two samurai. When they did they were surprised. No longer were the two horsemen a hundred yards back, but now rather three or four hundred yards back. All knew that it wasn't because the samurai were being outridden.

'What does it . . . mean?' Oboko asked uncertainly, but he too found himself smiling. He felt as if the clouds had suddenly lifted.

'Great toes of Buddha,' said Izzi, grinning. 'Death must have decided I was so ready he'd let me go for a while and wait until I was sleeping again.'

'Fool,' said Lord Arishi.

As the four watched, the two distant horsemen turned their horses and moved away, disappearing in an instant behind the rise. They did not reappear slightly to the left, which was the only way down; they did not reappear.

'But why turn back?' asked Oboko, still smiling.

'Who cares?' said Izzi. 'I'm sure as death not going to ride back and ask them.'

'Fools,' Lord Arishi said again, still staring at the rise behind which his two men had disappeared.

'Why "fools"?' Oboko asked and he turned to look at the eyes of Matari, which like those of her husband remained where they had been. Although she was no longer smiling, her eyes were glowing, attentive, her face wet with perspiration from the hard riding, black strands of hair matted down one side of her forehead and cheek. But even as he watched her, he saw a shadow cross her face as if some thought or memory had screened out the sight of her vanished pursuers. Her eyes and face cleared again, but she kept staring upwards.

'Yes,' said Lord Arishi softly, and as he did Matari's face paled and, lips trembling, she looked blankly at Oboko and then to the earth. As if to comfort it, she began stroking the neck of the stallion.

Oboko turned to look at the rise and there, immobile, stood the two horsemen and beside them stretching to right and left ten, twelve, perhaps fifteen other horsemen, all etched against the grey sky like so many twisted stumps of trees.

'Oboko,' Matari said sharply. 'Take Lord Arishi's horse, make him ride the grey. On three good horses we may still beat them to Lissa.'

'You might,' said Lord Arishi, without stirring. 'But you notice they have at least three riderless horses up there, many times as fresh as yours.'

'Get off!' Matari commanded. 'Izzi, go!'

Uncertainly, Izzi turned his horse and trotted around the fallen pine. Lord Arishi and Oboko slowly dismounted and, exchanging one ambiguous glance, each remounted the other's horse. Matari swung the black stallion around, dug in her heels and swept quickly away behind Izzi. Lord Arishi spurred the grey after her, and Oboko followed. The last two trotted through the shrubs around the base of the fallen pine and then back on to the muddy trail on the other side.

At first Oboko held his white horse behind that of Arishi, but when he saw how slowly the tired grey was moving, he spurred his own mount into a gallop to pass around Arishi on the left. Looking forward, he saw Matari's big stallion galloping across a long clear space, mud flying and then—as if it followed logically—an instantaneous blur and bump from the right and the ground was looming up at him, smashing him into temporary blackness.

For a brief moment he lay dazed in the mud before he pushed himself up to see what had happened. His and Lord Arishi's horses lay tangled and scrambling a few feet behind him, and Arishi, one leg pinned, lay against them. Oboko saw that he must have fallen over the neck of his falling horse and slid in an ungraceful muddy slide a dozen feet away, both his legs escaping uncrushed. Arishi, he realized, had swerved his horse in front of his at the last moment and caused the fall.

Oboko got to his feet and stumbled back to pull his white horse free. After yanking twice on the reins he knew that it wasn't tangled with the grey; the white horse was lame; his right foreleg would bear no weight. The grey was partly trapped; Oboko's horse on one side of him, Lord Arishi on the other. Looking back up the trail, Oboko could see, beneath the distant ridge, a long line of horsemen descending rapidly towards him—a few minutes away.

With all his strength he managed finally to haul the crippled white mare a few feet off the other and then to free Lord Arishi, who seemed in pain. The exhausted grey failed to rise but lay on the ground breathing heavily.

Mud splattered on Oboko's already mud-caked clothing and he turned to see Matari, wild-eyed and angry, above him on the rearing black stallion.

She looked at Oboko, who stared back blankly, at the two collapsed horses, and at Lord Arishi, who smiled at her.

'Careless of me,' he said simply.

She looked up at the trail, as did Oboko, and there they could just see a last horseman gallop out of sight behind a bend coming towards them. Izzi now arrived.

'Across the gorge,' Matari said. She leaped from her horse and half ran in strange unfeminine strides back up the hill. Oboko ran after her up the slope to the fallen pine and the edge of the gorge. Eighty feet below them the water roared and slammed over the rocks. The long pine, lying still and peaceful across the abyss, was thick for most of its length, narrowed near the other side, but could certainly support their weight. After a moment's hesitation, Oboko pulled himself up on to the trunk and reached back to help Matari. After he'd pulled her up beside him, her fingers remained digging into his arms where she'd held him while being lifted. Her eyes showed fear and bewilderment. She shook her head and gave a strange smile.

'I ... I'm afraid of this kind of ... height,' she said.

Oboko stared back.

'Go first,' she went on. 'I ... I'll look only at your back, at your heels.'

He turned and slowly, one behind the other, they began to walk out on the trunk of the fallen tree across the gorge. Below them was only the wild white rush of water. On each side of them as they crossed stretched out either a random green arm of the tree or ... emptiness. The thickness of the trunk and the frequency of strong limbs within reach permitted Oboko to walk out almost halfway before their becoming less thick forced him to go to his knees and crawl. Looking back over his shoulder, he saw Matari, who was also kneeling and staring at Oboko's heels, the figure of Lord Arishi coming towards them, and further back, still on the base of the pine, adjusting a bow on his neck, Izzi. A few hundred yards further up the side of the gorge, riding at full gallop, came half a dozen horsemen.

Oboko crawled forward. The trunk was still a foot wide in diameter here. Every three or four feet a strong branch sprouted outwards to provide a hand or foot hold. He was two-thirds of the way across. They were all crawling now, single file, a column of ants seeking escape above the white flames of the torrent. Oboko was at last within ten feet of the other side of the gorge, which, since he didn't dare raise his head to look at it, was represented by the wet brown earth he could just note on the rim of his vision. The trunk his two hands pressed against as he crawled was here only six or eight inches in diameter; what few limbs there were seemed too weak to support his weight. Still, unhesitating, he crawled onwards, barely balanced, a knee slipping off an inch once—his body trembling fiercely for a few seconds afterwards—then on, now only six feet to go. Then five, four, three ... He pulled himself into the crevice of the two large rocks and stood up. He was across.

Matari was within six feet of safety, her slender body white against the tree-trunk, her head lowered in concentration above the roaring explosions of water below. Lord Arishi was only a few feet behind her, Izzi many yards yet further back. Directly across from Oboko, silently watching, stood a line of half a dozen samurai. With Lord Arishi in danger, they were not shooting at Izzi or Oboko, but were sitting on their horses like a group of generals reviewing a parade.

But Oboko now realized that Matari was still five feet away and had stopped crawling. Her head still lowered, she knelt there immobile. He braced himself with one knee in the crevice so that he could reach far out and steady her the last four feet. Seeing beneath her frozen body the torrential flow of water and becoming aware of its great roar, he suddenly felt the terror he knew she must be feeling at the removal of the steadying sight of his boot-heels.

'You must crawl,' he said to her in a low, urgent voice.

Without looking up at him she began again to move, six inches forward, then a full twelve, and as Oboko stretched out an arm towards her, she looked up, started to reach for Oboko's hand, saw it was too far, and lost her balance: a hand, arm and shoulder sliding off the side of the trunk, the other clutching a small limb, her whole body off, one boot clinging a few seconds and then—it happened so quickly for Oboko that it was like the sudden incongruous appearance of a puppet—she was dangling downwards full length over the abyss, her fingers alone her last connection with the thin trunk, one hand grasping a single inch-thick branch, her other digging into the trunk itself.

Oboko, frozen, horrified, stared. Just three feet beyond the thin fingers of Matari clutching the dark bark of the tree Lord Arishi continued to crawl forward, his eyes also affixed on the trunk. Oboko watched as Arishi crept within a foot, then six inches, then a single inch of Matari's helpless fingers. He felt an impulse to draw his sword, to scream at Izzi who, as if unseeing, continued also his slow forward movement, still a good twenty feet beyond, hampered apparently by the bow running across his back.

For a long moment the large dark hands of Lord Arishi and the tiny fingers of Matari remained side by side, separated by a single inch of bare brown bark. Then Lord Arishi's right hand left the trunk of the tree.

Oboko watched in numbed fascination the large brown hand move towards the strained white hand of Matari, who, now, for the first time since she had slipped, leaned her head back to look up, her eyes meeting, without hate or hope or fear or appeal, the eyes of Lord Arishi. His dark hand enclosed a white wrist and with a sudden jerk he tore her hands away from the tree.

Matari gasped; Lord Arishi, his huge right arm trembling, lifted her twisting body upwards a full foot—her other hand now clawing for a hold on his wrist—then raised his head and looked directly at Oboko.

It was a strange expression, neither proud nor defiant nor frightened; it was almost a puzzled look. After holding Matari for another two or three seconds wriggling above the torrent like a rabbit held helpless by the ears, he straightened out his arm to try to hand her to Oboko. With one hand digging into an indentation in one of the boulders, Oboko leaned outwards over the gorge and grasped Matari's other thin wrist. For a single second both men held her there helpless and then Lord Arishi released her, himself collapsing forward on the narrow trunk and Matari swinging into the side of the gorge with a thud before Oboko had the strength, with her feet digging upwards against the earthen bank, to raise her to him. There the two of them clung to each other, trembling, unable to think or move, while Lord Arishi, recovering his balance, began again his relentless movement towards them.

In another minute all four of them were safely through the two boulders and standing solidly and stunned on the firm earth across from the now twelve samurai sitting silent on their horses on the opposite bank fifty feet away. The two lines of humans stood looking at each other thus for a full minute, until, as it had been building up to do all day, the grey sky released the first heavy wet drops of rain. Oboko, having held Matari against himself as if to shield off the enemy or whatever it was that had them both so trembling, released her at last and turned to face Lord Arishi and Izzi and the rain and the awful, relentless, uncertain, future.

Fourteen

It rained. At first tentatively, as if uncertain of its intentions, and then gently, as if wishing only to let the spring buds and wild flowers sip at an afternoon tea. After fifteen minutes it began to fall steadily, to create little rivulets in the bare earth, puddles in the low spots, fresh streams cascading lightly over rocks down into the gorge; and at last heavily, torrentially, blindingly.

Ended was the silent confrontation across the gorge, pursued and pursuers staring across at each other as spectators might at some natural disaster. Izzi, Matari, and Lord Arishi had left on foot, horseless, foodless, wineless, but alive, through a forest without trails, only rivulets of mud; without shelter except an occasional jutting rock or small cave; without signposts, only the unerring revelation of down.

Oboko had remained behind at the crossing of the gorge. When the rain was still only isolated drops from the heavy sky, Matari, Izzi and he had had to decide how to prevent the samurai from crossing after them on the fallen pine. They couldn't hack through the end of the pine to try to send it toppling into the gorge because bowmen from across the gorge would kill anyone who appeared in the crevice to try. Lord Arishi and Ignoto had exchanged a few words above the roar of the cataract which made it clear that as soon as that conversation was over the battle was on. Their only weapon, the three concluded, was the bow which Izzi had rescued from his brown gelding—he'd been looking for saki, he claimed—and Oboko was the only one who could shoot it accurately. He would have to remain as a threat to any samurai who tried to cross. His task was complicated by his having only one arrow, the others having either fallen into the gorge as Izzi crossed, or else never having been stuffed into Izzi's belt in the first place—Izzi couldn't remember. Oboko would have to remain; the other three would head directly down as close to the gorge as possible without being seen by the samurai, some of whom would be riding down on the other side. If the rain increased and began to wash out their trail they would find a hiding place and watch for Oboko; then all would continue together or hide together.

One arrow. After the three others had left, Matari leading Izzi and behind them Lord Arishi limping badly, Oboko was left crouched behind a rock back among the trees twenty feet from the edge of the gorge and about forty feet downhill from the fallen pine. He could see clearly the whole length of the tree. Although a shot would here and there be obscured by branches, he would have five or six clear ones before any samurai could crawl across. With one arrow.

On the other side of the gorge, six samurai had already ridden off southwards at full gallop. Another eight or nine now remained across from him. They knew where Oboko was and that he had a bow and arrows. Did they know how few arrows? Oboko assumed they didn't. The samurai, two still mounted, the other six or seven on foot, were clustered a few feet from the base of the fallen pine, in the open, as if contemptuous of Oboko's art as an archer. Actually, Oboko decided, they knew that he would not gratuitously kill unless one of them fired first or tried to cross the gorge after Lord Arishi and Matari. Oboko knew that at least two of the samurai had bows.

So Oboko half leaned and half crouched against the rock, his head and shoulders visible to those across from him. He could feel water sliding cold down the side of his neck but felt too tired to wipe it away. The steady roar of the mountain torrent below him enclosed his thoughts. The image of Matari's large brown eyes as she dangled from Lord Arishi's hand over the abyss, eyes as passive and innocent as those of a lamb awaiting the judgement of the butcher, flickered and faded in his mind. How different from the wild Matari that drove the black stallion as if he were the tamest pony, or the Matari, bright-eyed, laughing, who sang and joked and flirted as if life were a casual drawing room comedy. Or the Matari soft, helpless, in tears. Thinking of her warmed him, held at bay the uncontrollable trembling he could feel lay potential, a thought away, in his chilled, wet body.

When he felt the rain increasing and knew the samurai would have to act quickly, he shivered: in such thoughts lay the defeat of his body. His eyes on the figures across the gorge, his mind created the image of Matari as he had held her crying against him the evening before; warmth returned. And finally, just her eyes, brown earths in white space, bright, loving, only her eyes looking at him, competed with the thunderous bombardment of the raging water in the gorge below.

Then he saw. The subtle change of rain into a fine steady drizzle had spurred the samurai to action. Three horsemen galloped back upwards along the gorge. The five remaining—there seemed to be only five—took up protected positions, mostly on the far side of the fallen pine from Oboko. One, a bowman, stood mostly hidden behind a rock. As Oboko watched him, he notched an arrow and raised his bow, aiming directly at Oboko, who, instinctively but without fear, shrank down a few inches, curious. Then—Oboko wasn't really aware that anything serious was happening—an arrow ripped past his left ear so close he felt the feathers had touched him. Hearing the arrow thud into a tree a few yards behind, Oboko collapsed behind his rock.

Living Buddha: Izzi's dwarf had just whispered in Oboko's ear. He felt first numb, then resentment at the samurai for daring to come so close to killing him. The men opposite seemed suddenly to be madmen, murderers; he felt a strong urge to leap up and lecture them. Instead he peeked around the edge of his rock. Just as he'd been able to locate the archer again—he'd changed his position—a second arrow zinged past his right ear, this one missing by a full two inches, and hissed into the undergrowth beyond. Worse, Oboko had noted out of the corner of his eye a terrible thing: a man was already a third of the way across the fallen pine.

Fingers awkward and trembling, Oboko notched his single arrow. To make an accurate shot he would have to stand; to stand for no matter how short a moment would mean to be dead. Oboko sat. He would have to wait and shoot from a cramped position behind the rock, his left arm out as an unintended target for the bowman across the way, but the rest of him, he hoped, hidden.

An arrow twanged against his rock. He could only see the last third of the fallen pine on his own side of the gorge. Over that space of approximately fifteen to twenty feet he would have two exceptionally clear shots. The crawling samurai would then only be forty feet away; even cramped as he was, it would be a simple shot. He would have to kill the samurai.

'Go back!' he shouted impulsively to the figure he didn't even dare to see.

'Izzi!' a voice shouted to him as if in reply from across the gorge.

A truce? Oboko started to peer over the top of the rock but instead put down his bow for the moment and raised at one end of his arrow a piece of torn cloak. When he'd raised it six inches over the rock it was ripped away by an arrow.

His body was trembling uncontrollably now. He had an image of himself spending the rest of his life crouched here behind this rock, listening to the roar of the torrent, feeling the steady rain on his face, with arrows zipping, hissing, and twanging all about him into eternity. A samurai, crawling, was twelve feet away from Oboko's side of the gorge and the protection of the crevice where the pine tree ended.

Oboko and the crawling man were actually staring at each other. He had to pick up his bow again and re-notch his arrow. The samurai, blinking once, put his head down and began to inch forward again.

'Go back!' Oboko shouted at him, but even as he spoke he realized that there was no going back for anyone.

He drew back the arrow, his left hand outstretched under the falling rain and the samurai's thigh resting at the end of his arrow. Oboko was no longer trembling. An arrow tore through the cloak around his wrist carrying his left arm a few inches to his left and forcing him to redraw the bow and fill again the end of the arrow with the crawling man who, impossibly, was now mostly hidden beyond the one last bulky branch. Oboko quickly withdrew his arm. He'd have only one more chance. If he missed, he felt Matari would be doomed. He too, of course. If he struck, the samurai was dead. And then ...?

He watched the man, bunched and brown like a small bear, slowly emerge into the last six feet of open area, right where Matari had fallen. Holy Buddha, Oboko thought, what a man to crawl thus in the rain sixty feet with an arrow aimed at him, and crawling for what? For whom? Yet another arrow whished past a foot in front of Oboko's protected face. He immediately drew his bow, arrow, and enemy into a centred unit and shot, the samurai on the tree grunting once at the thud of the arrow into his thigh and toppling off the tree trunk to cling with his hands, dangling, where only minutes before, it seemed, had been Matari.

Short, unshaven, he hung down immobile and silent, looking without expression at Oboko, the arrow sticking all the way through his left thigh and with its point scratching harmlessly against the inside of his right thigh. Oboko heard shouts from across the gorge, whose noise seemed to have increased.

Oboko looked away, at the earth in front of him, and then, quickly, briefly, out at the whole stretch of the pine across the gorge. No one else was trying to cross. The samurai, helpless, alone, his legs without strength, no Lord Arishi to rescue him, hung a few moments more—Oboko without looking at him was watching—and then dropped, disappeared, into the abyss.

The rain was falling steadily now, occasionally blurring Oboko's vision as he tried a second time to peek across the gorge, an arrow rushing past him several inches away. It was time to go. He ducked down, propped his bow so that the top of it could just be seen and began crawling backwards away through the pine needles and mud, trying to keep his movement hidden from the other side of the gorge, knowing his life depended on it as well as the chance to delay the samurai from crossing. But already the rain was falling so hard that perhaps even without the threat of an arrow the danger of crossing the slippery tree trunk might be too great for them. Oboko didn't know. When he had backed down a small incline away from the gorge he stood up and began trotting down to find Matari. And Izzi.

And Lord Arishi.

Since the rain made it difficult to see any tracks as he ran and slid down, he shouted every thirty feet or so, wiping the water from his eyes, looking for some sign that they had passed, but seeing only pine needles, pebbles, rocks, and mud, streaming rivulets of mud, sliding with him downwards.

He had been running and slithering only ten minutes, it seemed, when he heard in reply to one of his shouts an answering shout, a bit behind and to his right. He scrambled up in that direction, barely able to see, shouted again, and at last saw Matari standing in the rain against a cliff-face. He climbed up to her and they embraced, clinging to each other in the rain.

After they had held each other thus for fifteen seconds—Oboko able to see past the wet blackness of her hair no more than a wall of falling water—she gently released herself and led him towards the face of the cliff. There she ducked down and entered beneath a long low rock ledge which jutted out over a stone floor. As Oboko followed her, he saw that the two rock formations stretched out about twenty feet with only four feet between them: a kind of open mouth in which sat, wet and exhausted, Matari and Izzi, and, at the upper end, Lord Arishi. Their shelter was partially hidden by shrubs and by the rain. As Oboko collapsed back against the rock wall beside Izzi in the middle of the long open mouth, he was dimly aware that the rain was now so thick that the hunt was for the time being over, until the next dawn perhaps.

They all sat, backs against rock, protected from above by rock, looking out at a fall of rain so violent and heavy that they might have been behind a waterfall. What wind existed was driving the rain from right to left in front of them so that, although their sheltered area was only three or four feet deep in most places, the only new wetness they suffered was from a gradual ooze which crept along their rock roof from the outside inwards and dripped, sporadically, down upon them.

Oboko lay back wet and cold, his thighs aching from the endless riding, his knees from the crossing of the pine, his arms from the unaccustomed handling of the bow and his frequent falls. He could barely listen to Izzi describing Lord Arishi's demonic ability to limp down, grimacing, through the rain and mud after him and Matari, even though the two of them had abandoned him when they saw how painful was his leg that had been injured in the fall of the horses. Instead Oboko stared with half-closed eyes at the thick wall of rain, listening, numbed, to the roar it made as it pounded the earth, trees and rocks hidden somewhere out beyond. On the little ledge he noticed a few pebbles, ants, some twigs, and animal droppings, but not enough wood to start even a tiny fire. There was nothing to be done. And so he sat back against the rock staring at the curtain of rain, feeling as if he were a part of an audience waiting between acts for the curtain again to lift.

Fifteen

Oboko dozed. Or partly dozed. And dreamed. Or at least reality took on dreamlike qualities. Just after his arrival, as Izzi talked, Oboko had looked past him once at Matari, who lay back against the rock wall with her eyes closed, her hair, face and body wet, her dress splotched with brown stains and with the black strands of hair which spilled down it in front. Then, even before Izzi had finished speaking, Oboko had let his chin fall forward on to his chest and closed his eyes. The sound of the rain pounding the earth a few feet away soon buried Izzi's words and again he tried to warm himself with the image of Matari, of her eyes. He may have slept, at peace with those eyes attending him. They seemed to sail through the grey sky of their long day, float serene on the white turbulence of the cascading torrent, lie in peace on the green valley they had seen beckoning them below.

His semi-sleep was broken once. He had a vivid image of Lord Arishi's great sword—a part of him recalled it must have been left behind on one of the horses—lying on the green grass as it might have lain on some silk pillow: it seemed on display. Though the brilliant silver sword was beautiful against the vivid green of the grass, the image, interrupting the flow of Matari's eyes, chilled him. He pulled his damp cloak closer to him and shivered; he tried again to re-create Matari in his mind to dispel the cold realities which kept intruding.

Although he hadn't been in the shelter of the rock more than twenty minutes he again seemed to sleep, blackness gathering and smothering him, until the voice of Izzi beside him began lazily to enter his consciousness. What Izzi was saying Oboko couldn't seem to bother himself to discover until he became aware that in the pauses Matari was sometimes speaking too. Oboko's hearing immediately began to stretch out through the six feet of the encircling sound of rain to pick up and translate her voice, clear, soft and serene it seemed to him in the blackness of his closed eyes and dream-world dozing. They must have been talking quietly for several minutes before any of their words finally penetrated Oboko's mind and were recorded. After a long shattering roll by the rain on the drums of the earth, it was Matari's voice which first broke through into remembered reality. Or was it a remembered dream?

'... I ... thank you,' she was saying in a low voice to Izzi.

And then the sound of the rain came: as if water were being turned on and off after and before each series of words.

'Only a poet gathering material,' Izzi replied after a while.

The sounds of the rain.

'I don't know why you've done ... what you've done,' came Matari's voice, even softer than before.

Again Izzi didn't reply for many seconds.

'I don't know why either,' he said, his voice a little more serious than Oboko remembered it usually being. 'I just seemed to do one thing and then another until ... I'm here.' There was the brief falling of rain. 'Actually,' he went on, 'I'm a hero. A great poet, magnificent lover, and a hero. Except for my stinking breath, which I have only when I'm drinking which is only all the time, I'm about perfect.'

Matari's laughter could just be heard within the rain.

'I wonder,' she said, more clearly now, 'what would have happened if ... if Lord Arishi had not ... been Lord Arishi, and you had become our court poet in Samika.'

'If I'd become court poet ...' Izzi said slowly, 'your

husband would have caught me ... being kind to you, you'd have had to flee to the mountains alone, and you and I would never have met.'

It was a strange sentence and the only response to it for many seconds was the rain, but then over that sound, or in it, Oboko heard them both laughing. And after a while, Matari's reply:

'Yes. If we'd met as lady and court poet in Samika, never would we have met. Or I and Oboko. And thus ...'

The sound of rain.

'You know,' came Izzi's husky voice, 'I wrote a poem about you today.'

'Yes?' said Matari.

'I wrote it in my head an hour ago while I was crawling across that tree trunk looking down into the gorge waiting for an arrow to come out through my belly.'

In the rain the sound of Matari's laughter.

'That's when you wrote it?'

'I always write best when I'm free of distractions,' he said. 'The poem's about you though, I think. I don't know what it means. Meaning I always leave to the scholars. It goes like this.' There was a brief pause and then Izzi's voice came in recitation:

> There: white abyss.
> Here: white butterfly on the pine trunk.
> Not much space between.

After the usual silence Matari commented softly: 'I'm not sure I like being called a butterfly ...'

'Maybe,' said Izzi in a strange voice, 'you're the white abyss.'

In the distance, over the sound of the rain pounding the earth outside, Oboko became aware he had just heard the rumble of thunder. Izzi's voice when it resumed was less theatrical than ever:

'When you've fallen off a precipice,' he said softly, 'and are only a few feet from the rocks, poetry and jokes are ... maybe ... in bad taste.'

The sound of rain curtailed their little play before Matari spoke:

'Yes?'

'I think that poem means ...' Izzi said slowly, 'among ... other things, of course ... that I love you.'

A silence lengthened, barely punctuated by the distant murmur of thunder. A single drop of water struck the back of Oboko's neck from the rock roof. So intent on Matari's reply was the awake-dreaming Oboko that he no longer heard the rain.

'What it means I guess,'—but it was Izzi's voice which broke the silence, a voice whose tone had changed completely, louder, harsher, the old Izzi—'is that I've been snowbound too long. I need a good fuck.'

There was a pause: absolute silence as Oboko remembered it but of course the rain still fell. This time Matari did reply.

'Yes,' she said quietly. 'Yes. That too.'

It couldn't really have been a dream; dreams were much more distorted, but so tired was Oboko that he must have slept for a few minutes on either side of that dialogue, a dialogue to which he didn't respond then at all, but which sailed through the sky of his mind with the same serenity as the floating planets of Matari's eyes which he kept trying to hold there like warm stuffed toys against the darkness.

But it wasn't yet dark. When Lord Arishi suddenly spoke to him he opened his eyes, he saw it was still light: yet another hour to darkness. He twisted his body on to his left side so that he could face Lord Arishi, who, he saw, was crumpled up grotesquely at an awkward angle at the upper end of their ledge a few feet to Oboko's left.

'What?' said Oboko.

'You killed one, didn't you?' Lord Arishi repeated. His wide eyes were red; he seemed feverish.

'Yes,' he replied, looking forward out into the rain.

'He tried to cross on the pine?'

'Yes.'

Lord Arishi turned his head from Oboko to look slightly to his left, at the exact same piece of the curtain of the rain at which Oboko looked.

'A short man. Beardless,' he said.

'Yes.'

'Tapu,' said Lord Arishi quietly. 'Had there been no fallen pine he would have tried to leap across.'

Oboko looked back at Lord Arishi, whose weary eyes returned to his at the same time.

'Unfortunately,' Lord Arishi went on. 'Tapu ... *cared*. Hence, an error in judgement.'

Oboko didn't answer. He was abruptly aware of being hungry.

'Caring, of course, this I have not ... *taught* you before, caring has its place, we must all *care* about some things, it's just that at certain times the law, the game, the rules, the promises, the vows, the men we are, demand that caring be put aside and action be all.'

'I don't think you ever care,' Oboko found himself replying, holding Arishi's eyes in his own. Vaguely he thought he heard Izzi and Matari talking again behind him.

'Because I am going to kill Matari?' Lord Arishi asked, seeming a little surprised.

'The man who kills Matari, who would try to kill her, must be dead beyond caring.'

Lord Arishi straightened his injured leg and sat up more erect. He adjusted his mud-smeared and soggy cape.

'You, of course, *care* for her,' he said.

'Yes,' Oboko answered in a low voice.

Lord Arishi was now staring at Oboko fiercely.

'You ... *care*, but I, killing, cannot.'

'Yes.' Oboko became aware that now he was shivering with the cold.

'You, a tiny piece of turd that Matari has accidentally picked up on her heel while fleeing, *care*, while I, Lord Arishi, her husband ...' With a violent forward thrust of his head and torso Lord Arishi spat on to Oboko, the wet saliva striking Oboko's arm and side and merging with the wetness that already covered him.

'Perhaps—' Oboko began, still trying to hold Arishi's fierce eyes.

'Where were you all the years that Matari and I held court for a hundred samurai, lived together, sang together, slept together, rode together?'

'I think—'

'Where were you when *Shogun* visited Samika, and Matari, third in the royal procession so stunned the massed crowds with her grace and beauty that the *Shogun* kept looking behind, wondering what fire or accident behind him caused the gasps and sighs of his subjects?'

'That's vanity,' said Oboko shrugging, 'I—'

'And where were you when Matari, glowing, ecstatic, gave birth to my son?'

The thunder rumbled again in the distance as Oboko, stunned into silence by the question, barely held his eyes where they were.

'And where were you when that son was carried into our room with his head broken and crushed like a mashed melon and she and I clung to each other in the darkness?'

'I was where I was,' Oboko finally answered desperately. 'But now I am here and I care and Matari shall not die.'

'And where were you,' Lord Arishi went on in a lower voice, his eyes still red and fierce, 'when the whispers began, the sidelong looks, the sudden fear in the faces of courtiers who before had looked at me only with love and awe?'

'There are always whispers ...'

'And then, at last, so new, so unexpected, so incredible that one thought it must be snakes hissing ... the snickers.'

'When a man is great, or a woman, there are those who joy in demeaning.'

'But *I* am an honourable man and my wife, by definition, an honourable woman, so I simply went to her and said, "Beware Matari, the fleas hop and bite about you and Lord Tariku."'

Now Oboko waited without words for the tale to toll through to its end.

'And she looked at me,' Lord Arishi went on, his fierceness gone, and on his face only his effort to remember correctly, truly, 'wide-eyed, serene, beautiful—as always beautiful, as even now,' he looked past Oboko down the length of the rock ledge towards her, Oboko not turning, 'as even now, wet, in rags, besmeared with muck, she is beautiful—and replied to me, "I shall beware."'

And now the curtain of rain which was falling less thickly seemed to Oboko not the fallen curtain of a drama at intermission, but rather the flicker and bright haze made by the theatre's lighted torches which blind the actors from the audience which sits watching them a few feet beyond.

'"I shall beware," she said, and smiled at me. Smiled at me. "Lord Tariku is your samurai," she added. "Send him away." But I do not dismiss samurai for whispers or lies; I do not dismiss samurai and thus humiliate beyond redemption myself and my wife, no, never that, never, I simply speak, giving truth and expecting truth, for when truth ceases, honour ceases, the world collapses and we are pigs rutting in the mud.'

Lord Arishi had returned his eyes to Oboko and the tears Oboko thought had formed briefly were no longer there; his face was haggard but expressionless.

'But then ...' he went on slowly, meditatively, 'the looks of fear in the faces of my servants became averted looks of shame, the hidden hissed snickers became blatant mocking laughter, always of course off to the side, indirect, explainable in terms of some other source, but obvious ... And I ...' (he seemed to be ploughing determinedly through to the end) 'patient, unjealous, trusting, did not lift a finger to test her faithfulness.' He paused briefly. 'But one day, having casually seen her riding on her horse Konlo in the distance southwards away from the city, I asked her much later where she had been and she told me she had been that afternoon in the carriage to the bookshop. Thus I knew she lied.'

As Lord Arishi paused for a moment, Oboko realized that in one sense that tiny little trip to the bookshop and the three words 'She had lied' were the end of the story for Lord Arishi. She had lied: her honour gone, she thus must die.

'As soon as she saw my expression at hearing her reply,' he went on, 'she knew I knew and—she still had honour of a sort of course—announced simply that she was leaving. No accusations of me, although we often fought in the past over her wild and unreasonable fancies, no apologies, no mention of Tariku or jealousy or marriage or vows or love, just: "I am leaving."'

Lord Arishi was silent, serene.

'Of course I couldn't let her leave—even alone, without any gentleman, even to disappear forever into some other life as she apparently planned, no, not that, never that, not that ever. No, of course, she had to die.'

'Let her go,' Oboko said quietly.

'Because Matari has ceased to be Matari, Lord Arishi does not cease being Lord Arishi. If she lives, all honour, all vows, become hollow. The whole world upon which I stand collapses. I kill, not because I do not care'—he looked fiercely at Oboko—'but because if I *don't* kill, then Lord Arishi would be dead and uncaring. Matari is the golden apple of the sun which, if it is not plucked quickly, rots into the worst stench of poisonous offal known to man.'

'You're mad,' Oboko said. 'She is not a golden apple, or a vow, or some sacred saint whose slightest sin must be burned away with a sword, but a woman, a human, and her death is senseless.'

'Her death is the only sense left me,' Lord Arishi answered looking away. 'If she lives, chaos would come.'

'Then let it come,' said Oboko.

'Blasphemy.'

'Better that than that you kill Matari.'

With a grimace of pain Lord Arishi bent his left leg back towards his groin. When the movement was completed the grimace altered naturally into a sneer.

'And it's been an interesting hunt, with worthy obstacles, worthy prey. The kill after such a challenging labour can only be beautiful.'

'It will be ugly, senseless, mad.'

'... beautiful and just.'

Oboko twisted his body in irritation and anguish and, turning to look past Izzi, saw ... emptiness. Matari was gone. For a moment he was carried back to the world of half-dozing and thought he must again be dreaming. Izzi sat back, eyes closed as if a wax statue.

'Izzi,' Oboko said. Reaching out, he shook his shoulder. Izzi turned his head and half opened his eyes.

'Where's Matari?' Oboko asked him urgently.

Izzi looked at Oboko a moment and then leaned back as he'd been and closed his eyes.

'Where is she?' Oboko asked him again sharply.

Without bothering to move himself in the slightest, Izzi answered lazily:

'Maybe she went to have a piss.'

Oboko crawled in front of Izzi and shook both his shoulders. Izzi opened his eyes.

'She's gone!' Oboko said.

'So you tell me.'

'You let her go!' he groaned in despair.

Izzi stared into Oboko's anguished eyes for a moment and finally replied:

'Some poems can only be written without words.'

Oboko looked out into the rain for a moment and then plunged through the curtain of the deluge and down through the mud. In the late afternoon light, under the dark sky and through the steady but lessening fall of rain, Oboko ran and slid down, able to see only thirty feet ahead of him, feeling as he ran an ache so great he felt he must scream forever and disintegrate if he couldn't find her.

He slipped and fell forward on to his hands and arms, cutting himself on a stone but rising as soon as he fell, raging, raging, raging against the rain, the mud, each pebble that slowed his way.

A hundred feet below the sheltered rock he'd left he shouted her name once, and ran on. As he stumbled between trees and rocks he found himself following a small eroded trail, rain splattering little brown explosions and washing mud and pebbles in a series of zigzag ruts. The way was clear of shrubs and rocks, but the wet earth slippery. Again he fell, rolling and rising again as if it were all part of a carefully rehearsed act.

As he ran down through the slanting rain, at last, ahead of him, running, he saw her. He shouted her name a second time, but she continued without turning down the washed out path. He increased his pace, each of his strides becoming as carefully calculated as a word in a poem. Within ten seconds he was close behind her, shouting her name a third time. While they were both still running downwards he reached out at last with his arms to grasp her, the very embracing causing them to fall together backwards and down, sliding through and into the mud, seeming to turn to each other even as they fell, so that Oboko saw just the briefest explosive image of her rain-stained, tear-stained, mud-stained face, eyes loving and hating and terrible, before their mouths met.

He pressed her body and mouth in maddened blissful effort to fuse Matari forever to him, never, ever to leave again. His love, doubt, grief and fear cascaded through him like four raging streams sinking together at last in ecstatic fall into the great sea they had always desired.

For a long moment they lay straining together in the mud under the rain, until Oboko felt that same helpless ache he'd felt while chasing her, only now free and flowing as triumphant need. Pushing himself a few inches out of her arms, he broke their kiss and clenched the wet, splotched white silk of her dress to tear it away from her, clawing at it, until he'd uncovered her, opened her, entered her with a great groan: an unquenchable log-clogged fire at last breaking white into ecstatic flame.

They kissed again, arms around each other, bodies locked, free at last. Twisting, groaning, unseeing of the twilight, unfeeling of the rain, unaware of the cold mud and pebbles in which they rolled, they exploded in an act of love which seemed to destroy everything which had ever existed before, only the white light pulsing, flowing, bursting, filling all. As their bodies writhed in the mud, the falling rain was striking down from the trees above where they lay and planting in the mud of the path and on the mud caked to their clothes and flesh the tiny white petals of cherry blossoms.

Sixteen

It was twilight when they regained consciousness of the world in which they lived. Their bodies and clothes were slimy with the mud in which they had lain and loved, and the rain was falling so gently now it only etched the caked mud without cleansing it. The approaching darkness, the mud, the chill dampness, the strange white petals that stuck to their flesh like insects, their act of love—something seemed to fill them with a vague dread. Wordlessly they adjusted their clothing, tried to wipe the mud from each other's faces and, hand in hand, retraced their steps upwards to try to find, before dark, the rock shelter from which they'd fled.

They walked slowly, glancing occasionally at each other, oblivious to the rain, but being driven back upwards to Lord Arishi and Izzi as if the four of them had become some kind of inseparable family. They had climbed two hundred feet when they saw, on a high ledge thirty feet in front of them and above, a figure standing, looking at them, outlined like a black angel against the withdrawing light to the west. It was Lord Arishi. They stopped, hand still in hand, and looked up at him. He was standing erect, serene and cold. For half a minute he looked down at them without speaking, and they, wet, dishevelled, with their bodies and clothes covered with mud, looked back. Oboko finally broke the long silence.

'Where's Izzi?' he asked quietly.

Lord Arishi, looming above them, responded slowly. 'While you were rutting in the mud,' he said, 'Izzi was writing a beautiful poem.'

'Where is he?' Oboko asked again.

'Here,' said Lord Arishi. His erect figure moved slightly and something moved at his feet and rolled off the ledge he stood upon, tumbling down the short incline and stopping, contorted and grotesque, at their feet. It was the body of Izzi, open-eyed, blood oozing yet from his slashed neck, and his intestines loose and uncoiled in the hideous open wound which had been his belly.

Too stunned and pained to speak, Matari and Oboko stared down at him until Matari collapsed forward on to her knees and let her face fall to Izzi's lifeless face. Oboko groaned aloud and fell to his knees beside her, touching with numb horror the wet hair and skin and looking at the unseeing eyes.

'The last death poem Izzi wrote was his best,' Oboko heard Lord Arishi saying from above him in an impassive voice, 'and he wrote it without words.'

Oboko looked up and, when he saw that cold judging face so confident of the principles with which it killed, he raised his two arms above his head and, with clenched fists, uttered a long, full-throated scream. All the rage, fear, bitterness, guilt, and hatred in his system poured into the scream until, breath exhausted, he let his body fall limp and he stared again into Izzi's absurd lifeless eyes.

They had found what they had somehow dreaded, and, having found it, had nowhere now to go. Oboko reached to touch Matari on the shoulder and raise her with him to her feet. She was crying. Her head was still bent with eyes on Izzi until, as Oboko tried to lead her gently away, she resisted his pull and looked up at Lord Arishi.

'Always,' she cried to him, 'your honour means death.'

As rigid and immobile as a granite statue he watched them.

'And always,' he replied, 'your honour is nothing.'

'I will flee your justice until ...' she began but ceased, and, tears falling, she shuddered into Oboko's arms.

'Until my justice is done,' said Lord Arishi.

Seventeen

Oboko turned Matari away from Lord Arishi and the body of Izzi and guided her down again. It was almost dark. Although Lord Arishi was free and armed with Izzi's sword, when Oboko glanced back half a minute after they'd left, he saw the black figure still outlined against the sky where he had been, perhaps because of his injured leg. Lord Arishi's samurai had not yet located them; in the darkness and the rain, Oboko felt they would soon be safe again—for another several hours.

Hand in hand they walked rapidly down the muddy path they had run down earlier, past the spot where they had fallen, lain and loved—water already forming a remarkably clear puddle where they had lain—down to a cliff-face which forced them to choose between moving to the left back towards the gorge, or right up across rocks and through woods into a hill. They decided to move away from the gorge, slipping on the bare rock as they climbed and beginning to lose their sense of direction in the darkness. A distant flash of lightning—the first they had noticed of the day's storm—permitted them to see that the hill they were climbing was endless: they must, in fact, be forking back up the mountain they had descended. But in the third brief flash of lightning—the thunder sounded so distant it might have been the noise of some lazy god clearing his throat—they saw a cave. In a few more seconds they had climbed to its mouth.

Except for the occasional flash of lightning, the darkness was now complete, cloud, rain, and fallen sun all combining to end all light except that provided in fits and starts by the approaching storm. The cave was not high enough for them to stand in except at the very opening, but it went in twelve or fifteen feet and even at that shallow depth felt warm compared to the chill rain outside. After exploring the cave and finding it clean and dry, Oboko returned to Matari at its mouth and saw, when lightning flashed, that the shrubs and cherry and plum trees near the cave fell away into a small valley which they now overlooked. Then he turned to Matari and together in the blackness and in the brief flashings of light, they removed their boots and piece by piece, the muddy rags which had been their clothing. They had no food, nothing with which to light a fire, no cup to catch the falling rain, no blanket to lie upon, no dry clothes to cover their nakedness. Embracing each other at the entrance of the cave, they felt lacking in nothing.

Letting the cold rain wash down over them, they began to clean each other, each stroke both an act to remove a smear of mud and a caress. When blackness was all, each simply rubbed downwards with hands over the other's wet skin; when a brief flicker of light let them see, both would concentrate on a single spot until their combined caresses had rubbed it clean. When they had finished washing each other's bodies, Oboko stood behind Matari and ran his fingers like a fleshed comb through the long thick strands of her hair, she with her head tilted back for a moment and her face into the rain. He combed and combed through it, Matari turning and rolling her head. Her hair, so silk-like and soft when dry, was heavy and wet, and gathered and spilled in Oboko's hands like a slippery animal. When his fingers ached from the long stroking, they turned to each other, and gently, fingers touching lightly as if too much pressure might kill, they wiped each other's faces. For Oboko, Matari's face, only inches away, would dreamlike flash into existence with a sheet of the now bright lightning, then disappear to become only a softness against his fingertips, which seemed to tremble in the crack or rumble of thunder which soon followed.

The lightning and thunder flashed and crashed only yards away and the rain was sweeping against them, but they stayed there touching each other's faces long after the last traces of dirt had been swept away. Finally, they turned with their arms around each other and looked out over the small valley that was sporadically lit up and faced the thunder booming all about them.

Oboko felt neither cold nor hunger nor fear in those moments, only awe at the incredible universe he was inhabiting: everything seemed to be lightning, wind, rain and thunder, and a warmth and peace and silence unlike any he'd known before. As the spring thunderstorm faded off up over the mountains to the north, they gathered up their wet clothing and went at last into the cave, crawling like animals into their burrow, one behind the other into the deepest part. There they spread out all their clothing in one narrow heap and lay down and embraced. Their bodies joining flesh against flesh, mouth against mouth, flesh within flesh, they lay together on the wet rags and hard rock and made love in the blackness.

They made love in the blackness. From the time the storm disappeared half an hour after they entered the cave together until dawn they could not see each other, could not, eyes wide, see anything which was not as black as the world of sleep into which they drifted off and on through the night. So, too, had sound disappeared; for the rain, which like the snow a few days earlier had seemed eternal, had soon stopped, and the wind too. Being far from the gorge they could hear in the recess of their cave nothing at all of the outside world.

In the blackness each tone and touch from each to each became so magnified that Oboko's whispered sound 'Matari' would seem to fill the universe, or so too would the feel of her chill fingers and warm lips on his face and neck, so delicate in their bearing to him of her love. The night was a night of touch not words; for what words could be spoken of a past which stretched back only three days and seemed but horror upon horror, or of a future which stretched that far even?—and seemed to promise only a horror beyond those they'd already known? They had only the present and their bodies and their love, and it seemed at times that a single sentence about past or future would bring into their womblike cave the outside world, and chaos would come.

And so they flowed from black painful bliss to the black world of sleep, the few moments of consciousness between the two being spent in the most commonplace of questions and comments about the hardness of rock, the dampness, the eeriness of total silence, the comfort of each for each. Only a single thought separated itself from the others in all that time. At some moment during the night when Oboko was soaring in the miraculous world he was inhabiting, the thought struck him that Matari was revealing in her passion the same drive and skill in the arts of love as she seemed to show in everything else she did, but the chilling questions of 'how' or 'why', although briefly considered, soon melted away forever in the darkness: it seemed to him that with even the tiniest and most casual touches Matari was expressing a love which was beyond art or skill or pretence. His universe had room only for love; cause and effect, morality, the past, the future—these trivialities would simply have to wait for another day.

Eighteen

When Oboko regained consciousness of the outside world it was of a round bowl of light glowing from the opening of the cave like the mouth of some creature whose face stretched away into infinity on every side. He awoke shivering, his stomach rumbling with hunger and his throat parched with thirst. After Matari had stirred and sat up beside him, they crawled side by side to the opening and stood up.

They saw before them an absolutely new universe: the sun, already two hours aloft, spilled its splendour across the rim of the ridge opposite them on to the trees, blossoms, buds, and flowers, so that all was light. Cherry blossoms bloomed on a dozen trees nearby; in the tiny valley into and over which they looked, the world was green and white and pink and yellow and orange: all the colours of life ablaze in the early morning sun. In some archetypal reversal of the Christian story of Genesis they had eaten of the apple and seemed now to have been exiled *into* the Garden of Eden from the terrible earth they had been inhabiting. Half a dozen birds darted and swerved across their line of sight; others twittered noisily in some trees to their left. Looking south, Oboko could see that for the first time the green valley of Lissa opened out into a sea which was a bright and peaceful blue.

They looked at each other's nakedness not with shame but with curiosity: bodies which each had known with an intimacy of touch which needed no repetition to be complete, suddenly, in daylight, were new again, as if reborn. They laughed and shivered and hugged and smiled, stupidly, without thought, smiled and trembled, warmed by each other and the sun which, cupped by the shape of the hill around them, created a pool of warm light in which they bathed.

The earth was still wet. Grass, buds, leaves and flowers were all touched with tiny droplets which glistened in the light like random diamonds dropped during the night's storm. When the two had warmed away their shivering, they wandered out on to the moist earth, which oozed between their toes and slid under their bare feet as if they walked on the oils of love. There was no fruit, of course, but they picked grasses and flowers, and chewed and swallowed their moisture. They knelt on the earth and lapped at shallow puddles to drink the clear water before it muddied with the touch of their hands or feet.

When they looked about them they could see that the previous evening they had climbed up a dead end: to their left was a wet black cliff-face which permitted no further ascension. Across from them, the other side of their little vale was also steep. Although passable, Oboko knew it would only lead to the gorge on its other side. Up behind their cave was another black cliff. When they eventually came to move they could only go back down and along the gorge south to the valley of Lissa and the sea.

They climbed again to their cave and sat, naked, in the sunlight, their bodies, exhausted, relaxing fully for the first time since they had met. They sometimes talked, words falling with difficulty from lips numb and bruised from their long night's love. Of nothing they talked, past and future blocked in both. Only the shape of flowers, the feel of sun, the taste of grass in the mouth, were fit for words.

They tried to dry their clothes but, when an hour later they began to dress themselves, their rags were as damp and cold as the world to which they were at last slowly returning. Matari's white dress, the one she had worn in the snow up to the old temple, was no longer a dress but a collection of torn and dirty strips held tenuously together.

She and Oboko adjusted them over her body with intent seriousness. When they stood again in their boots and wet clothing and looked down into the distant valley of Lissa, they suddenly found themselves cold, hungry and afraid. Matari pulled a piece of the stained silk across the front of her as if to hide her nakedness.

They talked now of their plans, the old Oboko and the old Matari being thus reborn. They knew that to pass eastward over the gorge at the bridge would be impossible. To try to enter Lissa on foot, no matter what fields and thickets they might try to use, seemed equally dangerous. The only place of which their enemies might not think, where they might cross the gorge, was the sea coast itself. If they could get there undetected they might swim past the point where the gorge spilled out into the sea. Once east of the gorge they would be free. Of course, between their cave and the sea Lord Arishi and his samurai and perhaps peasants whom Lord Arishi had given money would be looking for them. Sooner or later, it was known, Oboko and Matari had to descend into the valley of Lissa. Lord Arishi, twenty years of hunting skills at work, would be waiting.

They went down.

Nineteen

Oboko had never been trained as a warrior. He had learned the rudiments of the arts of archery and swordsmanship before his decision that he must gain spiritual skills had sent him to Master Eno on Nuni Bay. There he had meditated upon the *koans* and *mondos,* listened to Master Eno's words, observed his life, and strived to obtain enlightenment. He had not yet experienced *satori* but the three years of discipline at the monastery had given him some ability to protect his thoughts and feelings from certain distractions, an ability which is part of the art of the successful warrior.

As he began walking down the mountain with Matari he knew that only thoughts and feelings relevant to saving their lives could be permitted. His love and fear for Matari must all be bottled and stored on the shelf of his mind until they were again appropriate for drinking. The reply of his senses to the beauty of the earth in spring had also to be controlled. He could not afford to see the brilliant white and pink of the cherry blossoms, the yellow green of the reborn grasses cascading down hillsides, the bright yellow and red of wild flowers diffusing their colours in the meadows.

Matari also had not been trained as a warrior, but like Oboko had been trained in arts whose principles of concentration had prepared her for the challenge she had been facing. At almost the same moment a few dozen yards below their cave each released the other's hand, as if love, their whole universe for fourteen hours, could no longer be permitted even that tiny part of the world which was the touch of hand to hand. Eyes which had been glowing narrowed to attention to each rock and rise and tree behind which a samurai might be awaiting them. And so they descended.

Matari walked ahead of Oboko, both of them assuming that Oboko might be killed without warning but that she wouldn't be. Tree, shrub, grass and flower bloomed and blossomed on every side of them, but they saw only places of danger, places free from danger. Since the slope downwards was now gradual they followed no trail but made their way without difficulty through the sparse woods and occasional meadow. They had been walking for almost two hours and had almost reached the floor of the Lissa valley when Oboko noticed that Matari had stopped and was looking up to her left. When she looked back at Oboko, her expression communicated everything.

Wearily, but without fear, Oboko drew his sword. Even as he did so a horse and rider walked slowly down a slight slope into sight and halted a few yards from Matari. Oboko continued to walk forward, noticing without emotion that the samurai had also drawn his sword, a long sword, and sat on his horse watching impassively Oboko's approach.

Both Matari's actions—she had scanned the hillside from which the horseman had come—and his own senses indicated to Oboko that this warrior was alone. Fifteen feet from the horse Oboko stopped.

'Lord Arishi wishes to see his wife,' the man said. He was tall and slender with a three day growth of beard and a scar across his cheek. His eyes were half-closed as if he were sleepy.

'No,' Oboko answered simply.

Matari was standing silently to Oboko's right about the same distance from each of the two men.

'Bashu,' she said. 'You may ride away and tell my husband where I am.'

The samurai kept his eyes on Oboko.

'My orders,' he said, 'are to bring you to Lord Arishi. And to kill anyone who intervenes.'

Oboko realized that this man on a horse with a sword a full foot longer than his was not a welcome opponent.

'And if we do not resist?' Oboko asked.

The samurai, still sleepy-eyed, his sword still hanging lifelessly from his hand down beside the right foreleg of his horse, hadn't moved since the encounter had begun. He replied:

'If you do not resist, I may kill you or not, at my pleasure.'

'And what is your pleasure this morning?' Oboko asked.

The horseman seemed to be examining him through his half-closed eyes as if Oboko were some new species.

'My pleasure,' he repled after several seconds, 'is for you to drop your sword and walk ahead of us to the Lissa road.'

'How nice,' said Oboko and suddenly sprinted across in front of the horse to be opposite the sword side of the samurai who, at the very instant Oboko began to move, seemed to spur his horse forward to block Oboko's way. The horse would have struck him chest to chest had Oboko not dived forward face first, the horse striking his hip and thigh and the samurai's sword slicing air just above his back as he passed.

As he scrambled to his feet and the horse wheeled to charge again, Matari stepped between the two. The horse reared and snorted, twisting his head. Shuddering and stamping, it was finally brought to a standstill by the horseman, who, his eyes still half-closed, but now breathing more rapidly, watched Oboko. For a moment they remained at rest in their new tableau. Then Matari walked forward up to the horse and alongside it to stand directly beside and even slightly against the boot and long sword of the samurai, who, unmoving watched Oboko.

'Get away from the horse, Lady Arishi,' Bashu said coldly.

'I will come with you,' she said softly.

The samurai's eyelids flickered as if in uncertainty.

'Get away from the horse,' he said again. 'I have changed my pleasure.'

'I will ride behind you,' Matari said softly and seemed to reach her small hand upwards towards the saddle.

'Get away from the . . .' Bashu began again, but suddenly jerked his gaze away from Oboko to Matari. As he raised his sword arm he lifted with it, Oboko saw with terror, the body of Matari who had grasped his wrist. Oboko charged, the samurai raised both his sword and the dangling Matari over his shoulder and, as the two men met, tried to strike down at Oboko, who parried the burdened blow and plunged his own sword above Matari's lowered form into the unprotected side of the horseman.

As the horse lunged past Oboko, the sword was drawn out of the body it had entered and Matari was dragged several yards before she released her grip and fell to the earth. The horse galloped forward a dozen yards before Bashu, now clutching his wounded side with the hand which held the reins, brought it to a halt. Still holding his great sword limply in his right hand, he slowly turned his horse to face them again.

Matari had risen to her feet and stood again between the two men, Bashu now with eyes wide open in a twisted pain-filled grimace; Oboko, sword bloodied six inches to the point, silently waiting. After watching Oboko for a few moments he turned his eyes for the first time on Matari; he appeared to be examining her as he had earlier looked at Oboko. Eyes half closed, he seemed like a scientist squinting through a microscope. Then, with his face now impassive but still clutching his side, he turned the horse about and set it away at a trot south towards the Lissa road.

As soon as he disappeared around a little hillock, Oboko and Matari, warriors still, headed rapidly off to their right. They were far enough down in the valley now even to head towards the city if they dared, but in any case were no longer funnelled by the feet of the mountains. They chose to stay in terrain as wooded and uneven as possible and to get quickly away from where they had just fought.

Within ten minutes they could see between the trees ahead of them a single thatched cottage and the Lissa road. They didn't hesitate: both instinctively felt they must cross it immediately, before Lord Arishi, hearing from the wounded samurai, had a chance to concentrate his men along it. As they moved out of the woods and began crossing a freshly ploughed field towards the road, they could see only one sign of life: well to their right a farmer was bent over the earth, planting. Seeing signs of civilization —the cottage, the man and the regular muddied ruts in the road—Oboko felt a strange self-consciousness, shame even, or guilt, as if he didn't belong here. Without looking at each other he and Matari hurried through the mud of the ploughed field, crossed the lesser mud of the road, and came into the grassy meadow on the other side. Within two minutes they were again free from the stares of the empty cottage and the oblivious man, planting.

Again in woodland they soon came upon a path which, after they'd followed it a few minutes, seemed to be leading them to the south and east, to the meeting of gorge and sea. They stopped to discuss whether they should follow the path or try to work their way through the woods. They decided to hurry ahead on the path; a horseman coming up behind them could be heard in sufficient time to hide, and they doubted that Lord Arishi had already placed men between them and the sea. They didn't know how many other paths might be running parallel to the one they were on. Safety seemed to lie in crossing the gorge, not in hiding. They hurried on.

As they went, Matari again leading, the woods became thicker, and the sun, although it was high in the sky, seldom broke into their path. They could see it flickering on the leaves on the tree tops, but where they walked it was shaded. They began to hear a strange 'shhshing' sound off to their left and realized after a few minutes that it must be the mountain gorge which they would soon again be meeting.

They had been walking more than forty minutes when ahead of them they could see that at last the woods ended and their path emerged out into a sunlit green clearing. In addition, above the sound of the torrent in the gorge out of sight to their left, they could hear ahead of them the rhythmic crashing of the breakers on the beach. They had reached the sea.

Matari, the remains of her white dress grotesquely and absurdly about her, walked straight out into the sunlight, head held high, heading across the green meadow for a tiny rise where the edge of the gorge met the edge of the sea. She looked to her right when she first emerged into the sunlight, then ahead again. Oboko, sword in hand, followed.

He too when he emerged into the sunlight looked about, first to his left where he saw thirty yards of woods stretching in a straight line to the edge of the gorge, then to his right he could see the meadow flowing off a hundred yards to a rise, and to the right and behind him as he followed Matari, the woods again, uneven here, with stretches of grass flowing in amongst the trees like green surf spilling among clusters of rocks. The only sounds were the roar of the mountain waters into the sea and the regular heavy gasp and wheeze of the ocean waves breaking over the stones of the beach below the meadow.

But even as he looked for signs of samurai and then ahead again to follow Matari's undeviating path through the sunlight to the meeting of gorge and sea, Oboko found himself smiling; he felt light, giddy, alive. The warrior was overwhelmed with the flow of a hundred unstoppered bottles: love, joy, the pleasure of sunlight on head and shoulders, the pressure of the moist grassed earth cushioning each step, the touch of the warm wind sliding effortlessly past his face, the sight of Matari's long black hair rising and falling ever so slightly down her back as she walked, and finally, as he came up and stood beside her, the look of the sea. As he sheathed his sword and gazed down at the bright blue water stretching off forever before them, the waves, rising and falling in great white splashes fifty feet below and in front of them, sprayed and sparkled and danced as if in special performance for them alone.

The waters of the gorge rumbled more deeply here where they buried themselves into the ocean. For fifty yards out from the shore Oboko could see the swift flow of water ripping through the passive sea. To swim across that submerged river without being swept out too far would be ... difficult. They would have to remove their clothes, immerse themselves in the water, fight the torrent, and—was it possible?—be reborn on the other side, naked, with nothing. Naked, with everything.

Without looking up at him, Matari turned into his arms. As he held her, the silk of her dress seemed in places to be dry at last, such warmth did the sun pour down upon them. Beyond her head, which was pressed to his shoulder, Oboko saw two sea gulls wheeling through the sky down and around and up again as if searching for something in the waters of the torrent flowing to the sea, something which wasn't there. Matari, her averted face also staring down at the rush of water they would have to swim, heaved a heavy sigh. Then they turned together to look back at the meadow they had crossed and saw in a little cove of sunlight back amongst the trees, seated lotus-fashion like some religious statue which had been there for centuries, his great sword across his lap, Lord Arishi.

On either side of him stood a samurai, one of whom held three horses. Lord Arishi was dressed in clean clothes: a black cape over dark pants. In the sunlight the only thing about his sitting there which was bright was the long sword which glittered above the pool of green grass as if it were on display.

Neither Oboko nor Matari started or trembled at seeing

Lord Arishi; his being there seemed, as soon as they'd seen him, to be inevitable. The idea of emerging naked and reborn and free on the other side of the mountain torrent they had watched pouring into the sea had apparently only been an enchanted dream. When Oboko turned to look at Matari she was looking up at him smiling, as if, even with the sword descending, there was happiness in sunlight warming bruised lips. She said simply:

'I chose, I bloomed ...'

She turned to face Lord Arishi, detached herself from Oboko, and began to stride across the meadow. Oboko, not yet reacting to what was happening, turned and followed. They marched in a straight line towards Lord Arishi—as if on parade. When Matari had reached within twenty feet of him, she halted. Lord Arishi, still seated in the lotus posture like a black Buddha, great sword unsheathed across his lap, looked at her without expression. Oboko stopped behind Matari and a few feet to the right. He was aware of birds twittering in the trees behind Lord Arishi.

'Could we borrow two horses?' he heard Matari ask unexpectedly. 'We wish to ride to the east.'

Lord Arishi didn't answer. He looked at her impassively. The two samurai who flanked him hadn't drawn their swords, but Oboko was aware that behind him and Matari and to their right other samurai also now stood silently watching.

'Also clothing and food,' said Matari. 'We have had a difficult journey.'

Oboko could only see her back and part of her right side: she was standing very erect, her hair spilling down her back, her dress in tatters. As Lord Arishi still stared at her without expression, Oboko realized that, without swords, the two of them were engaged in their last battle. The birds behind in the woods continued to sing.

'You must die,' Lord Arishi said in a hoarse voice.

'Why?' Matari asked clearly.

The question lay on the grass before them all for several seconds before Lord Arishi, still coldly watching his wife, spoke.

'I have judged,' he answered simply.

'I wish to live,' Matari said. She spoke so clearly, so firmly, so impassively, so absurdly, that Oboko wondered why she was speaking.

'I have judged,' Lord Arishi said again.

'Please let me and the poet Oboko go,' Matari said in her incongruously formal voice. 'We will cross the sea to China.'

Lord Arishi looked at her a moment longer and then at last shifted his eyes to Oboko.

'Leave us, little man,' he said. 'The wind calls you. It may not call again.'

Oboko closed his eyes for a second, why he did not know, opened them and slowly, heavily, drew his sword.

Lord Arishi's face remained neutral, impassive.

'Well then,' he said, 'thus it will end.'

Matari now turned slightly and spoke to Oboko.

'I thank you for accompanying me,' she said. 'Now, it is ... my desire ... that you leave.' Her eyes were meeting his warm and attentive, but controlled.

'As long as we both live, Matari,' he said to her, 'I will never leave.'

Matari continued to look at him warmly but somehow distantly, as if she were already far off and flying away at great speed.

'She is dead, Oboko,' Lord Arishi announced quietly. 'Don't bloody up the ground with your youth.'

'I wish,' said Matari softly, 'for the love you bear me and ... the love I bear you, that now ...' (wetness glistened in her eyes but her expression remained one of warm distance) '... that you would now put away your sword and leave.'

Seeing Matari close to tears, Oboko realized with the finality of the samurai's dropping into the abyss that she was about to be killed. With their quiet, controlled voices they were somehow all playing out the last act of a drama conceived by some madman. Nothing, nothing, nothing could justify the death of Matari. He turned from the moist eyes of Matari to face again Lord Arishi.

'You *can't* kill her!' he said harshly.

Lord Arishi met his anguished gaze with indifference and, moving for the first time since they'd seen him, placed his right hand on the hilt of his great sword and raised up the hilt until the point hung down vertically. Using the sword as a staff, grimacing slightly and favouring his left leg, he brought himself to a standing position.

'We can only see,' he said simply.

He straightened himself to his full height, his long unsheathed sword angling forward from his hand so that its point rested an inch above the ground two feet in front of him. There were leaves of grass sticking to the cloth of his pants where his knees had been resting.

Matari, still facing Oboko, spoke again, for the first time urgency entering her voice.

'No, Oboko, no,' she said. 'It is finished.'

'Let her go,' Oboko said grimly to Lord Arishi. 'Let her go.'

Lord Arishi, wordless, began slowly, incredibly slowly, to move, to limp towards Oboko, his eyes steady and controlled. When he had moved to within twelve feet of Oboko, Matari took two steps and stood between them.

'No,' she said, facing Lord Arishi. 'I am ready, my lord, to die.'

'Nobility in mud,' said Lord Arishi, stopping four feet from her.

'She shall not die,' Oboko said sharply, and moved to his right so that Matari was no longer between them. He was partly aware that all the way around behind him now was a circle of Lord Arishi's samurai. Matari, her husband and he now stood in a triangle, barely a sword's length separate from each other.

For several moments the two men looked at each

other, each standing with legs slightly apart, knees slightly bent, swords in their right hands, Matari between them to Oboko's left, looking at Lord Arishi.

'And now,' said Lord Arishi in a low voice, 'we shall end the play.'

'Niko,' said Matari softly, urgently.

Lord Arishi's face, for so long cold and impassive, flushed and tensed.

'Niko,' she said again softly. Oboko noting in a single swift glance that she was smiling. Smiling!

As if the sound of his intimate name coming from her lips reminded him of their warm moments together and of all he had lost, Lord Arishi in a movement so swift Oboko's body only twitched in response swept his sword sideways up and away and slashed through Matari's neck, toppling her body and severed head to the grass in a graceless heap.

Oboko stared down at the blood pouring from her neck as her heart perhaps beat on, at her eyes open and fixed, at her face ... smiling. Numb and unthinking he looked back up to face Lord Arishi, whose eyes were also open and fixed, staring through Oboko at nothing. Arishi's sword had returned mechanically to readiness, dripping tiny droplets of blood on to the grass. But with a sudden suppressed choking sound he bent back his head as if struck and writhed forward to fall on his hands and knees beside the body of Matari, his great sword toppling sideways to lie on the grass. His fists clenched before him as if his wrists were bound, Arishi crawled a few more inches and let his head and clenched fists fall forward on to Matari's dead flesh, his face buried in her dress.

Still stunned and numb Oboko stared for several more seconds at the two figures, the black kneeling over the soiled white. Letting his sword fall from him to the earth, he looked once more at Lord Arishi bent forward on his knees over the body of Matari as if in prayer, once more at the dim eyes staring out into infinity as if seeing all and the face smiling. Then he turned and walked away.

He walked towards the circle of silent samurai which had formed around them, between two of the men whose faces he did not look at and did not see, past the place where the trail he and Matari had taken that morning came out on to this little patch of green upon which she lay dead, across the meadow, past a cluster of horses moving nervously against each other as he passed, on to a well-trodden path, a donkey path, that led to the west towards the city of Lissa. As he moved slowly away from the sea he became aware of the songs of the birds and budding shrubs, and could hear in the distance ahead of him the shouts of children at play.

Death Poem*

Strange you did not touch me
Long ago
When cherry blossoms bloomed.
You seemed ugly to me then,
Black rider,
And I raged against your honourable thrusts.
Rage was right.
And yet tonight
I give you without fuss
My hand.
I chose;
I've seen the sun on wild flowers.
I have ridden the white wind.

1862, Oboko, 1772-1862

* This poem was written, according to legend, a few hours before his death at ninety, as he sat in the lotus posture surrounded by half a dozen disciples in the small country town (abandoned now) of Luchoko in northern Japan.

The flies, red-footed, gather to eat,
Get tangled in your hair.
Thus.

Oboko

On Entering My Coffin*

Well, I had to work hard to get here
And look,
The ants already patrol the grounds,
Awaiting the manna
Of me.

1794, Izzi

* This is one of six extant 'Death Poems' attributed to the poet Izzi, none of which were followed by his actual death. He is the only Japanese poet known to have written more than one.

Prayer to the Sun*

Opulent globe of lightning, cupped
In the invisible skin of god, spit
Your light upon us, flay
Our hides with your white whip, heat
Our flesh upon the griddle of your earth
And bake us 'til we rise
And are eaten.

1797, anonymous, attributed
to Lord Arishi, 1757-96

* Of the two dozen poems now generally attributed to Lord Arishi, this is the last, and the only one known to have been written after the death of his wife. Arishi himself was killed less than a year later in a battle with some obscure bandits far from his city of Samika.